ALSO BY MIDGE RAYMOND

Forgetting English: Stories

MY LAST CONTINENT

A NOVEL

MIDGE RAYMOND

SCRIBNER

NEW YORK   LONDON   TORONTO   SYDNEY   NEW DELHI

SCRIBNER

An Imprint of Simon & Schuster, Inc.
1230 Avenue of the Americas
New York, NY 10020

First Scribner hardcover edition June 2016

SCRIBNER and design are registered trademarks of
The Gale Group, Inc. used under license by Simon & Schuster, Inc.,
the publisher of this work.

For information about special discounts for bulk purchases,
please contact Simon & Schuster Special Sales at 1-866-506-1949
or business@simonandschuster.com.

The Simon & Schuster Speakers Bureau can bring authors
to your live event. For more information or to book an event, contact
the Simon & Schuster Speakers Bureau at 1-866-248-3049
or visit our website at www.simonspeakers.com.

Interior design by Kyle Kabel

Manufactured in the United States of America

1   3   5   7   9   10   8   6   4   2

Library of Congress Cataloging-in-Publication Data

Raymond, Midge.
My last continent : a novel / by Midge Raymond. — First Scribner
hardcover edition.
pages ; cm
I. Title.
PS3618.A9855M9 2016
813'.6 — dc23
2015033592

ISBN 978-1-5011-2470-9
ISBN 978-1-5011-2472-3 (ebook)

For John

My Last Continent

A s I lead tourists from the Zodiacs up rocky trails to the penguin colonies, I notice how these visitors—stuffed into oversize, puffy red parkas—walk like the penguins themselves: eyes to the snowy ground, arms out for balance. They're as determined as the penguins to get where they're going—but they're not here to ask about the birds, about these islands. They don't seem interested in the Adélies' declining populations or the gentoos' breeding habits or the chinstraps' dwindling food sources in the Antarctic.

Instead they ask about the *Australis*.

How many people drowned? they ask. *How many are still missing? How many bodies now belong eternally to the sea?*

None are questions I want to answer.

Back in 1979, a sightseeing tour, Air New Zealand Flight 901 out of Christchurch, crashed into the side of Mt. Erebus in southwestern Antarctica. More than two hundred and fifty people died that day. It was the worst disaster in the history of this continent—until five years ago. Until the *Australis*.

According to records, we know that both crafts—the plane and the ship—went down due to navigational error. Each was felled by what its crew knew existed but was unable to see, or chose not to see.

Sometimes I wonder whether some other force is at hand—something equally obscured, warning us that none of us should be in Antarctica at all.

We cross sharp-edged hills near penguin nests, the rocks covered with pinkish red guano that seeps into the snow like blood. At this time of year—late January, the middle of the austral summer—the birds are fat, their chicks tucked under their chests; they lean over to warm and protect the downy gray-and-white bodies as they watch us pass. The Adélies stare at us with their white-rimmed eyes; the chinstraps look serious in their painted helmets; the gentoos twist their heads, raising orange beaks into the air to keep us in their sights.

More than anything, the birds remind me of everything I've lost. And somehow, this only makes me more determined to save them. And so I return.

I'd prefer not to answer the tourists' questions about the *Australis*, but I do. This is my job, after all—I work not only for the penguins but for the boat that brings me here every season.

So I tell them.

I tell them I was here when the massive cruise ship found herself trapped and sinking in a windswept cove of pack ice. I tell them that the ship was too big and too fragile to be so far south, and that my ship, the *Cormorant*, was the closest one and still a full day's travel away. I tell them that, below the Antarctic Circle, the phrase *search and rescue* has little practical meaning. There is simply no one around to rescue you.

I tell them that 715 passengers and crew died that day. I don't tell them that 2 of those who died were rescuers, whose fates tragically intertwined. Most want to hear about the victims, not the rescuers. They don't yet know that we are one and the same.

ONE WEEK BEFORE SHIPWRECK

The Drake Passage
(59°39'S, 61°56'W)

From the motion of the M/S *Cormorant*, it feels as though we've hit fifteen-foot swells. This is nothing for our captain, who chugged through thirty-foot waves a little more than two weeks ago on a previous trip through the Drake Passage, where the Southern Ocean, the Pacific Ocean, and the Atlantic meet and toss boats around like toys. Though the *Cormorant* will make the voyage six times this season, it will never become routine. The Drake never gives the same experience twice.

I'm not nearly as seasick as I pretend to be, but the downtime helps me ease into my role as tour guide. Because 90 percent of the passengers are sick in their cabins and will remain sequestered for the next two days, our expedition leader, Glenn, doesn't mind if I hide out in the crew's quarters until we reach the South Shetlands.

The company's flagship vessel, the *Cormorant*, was built the same year I was born, nearly forty years ago. While I'm five foot nine and single, she is just shy of three hundred feet long and carries one hundred passengers and fifty crew members. We are both built for the ice—I've got a thick skin and a penchant for solitude; she's got stabilizers and a reinforced hull, allowing us to slip into the tiny inlets of the Antarctic peninsula and, weather permitting, to go south of the Antarctic Circle—something all visitors want to check off their lists of things to do before they die.

The promotional brochures for this cruise highlight not only the wildlife but the onboard experts like me. I'm one of six naturalists on this voyage—a group of wildlife experts and historians hired by Glenn to educate the passengers on penguins, whales, seabirds, ice, and the stories of the continent itself. While most naturalists will remain on board for the full two-week journey, several times each season two of us will disembark at one of the peninsula's uninhabited islands, make camp, and gather data for the Antarctic Penguins Project. After another two weeks, when the ship returns with a new load of passengers, we'll join them for the journey back to civilization. While I'm on the ship, I'm on call, available to answer questions, pilot Zodiacs (the small but sturdy inflatable boats that take us from ship to shore), herd tourists, spot whales, and give presentations in the lounge after dinner. This part I love—introducing the continent as it was once introduced to me. The part I dread involves the questions that venture far beyond the realms of flora and fauna.

At least once on every voyage, someone will ask me how I do it—how I can live for weeks or months at a time down here, going from ship to tent, dealing with the harsh conditions, spending so much time alone. They will ask whether

I'm married, whether I have kids—questions I rarely hear asked of a male naturalist. But because I want to keep this gig, I will bite my tongue and smile. I'll tell them I know penguin breeding habits well, but human connections are another thing entirely and are especially complicated when it comes to the Antarctic. I'll offer up a bit of the continent's history, overflowing with stories of love gone wrong: The polar scientist Jean-Baptiste Charcot returned home after wintering on the ice to find that his wife had left him. Robert Falcon Scott, who died on the continent, never even knew about the rumors that his wife had strayed while he was away. And of course I have stories of my own, from my complicated and still-evolving history of love on the ice, but these I'll never share.

The brochures also highlight the fine dining, the fitness center and sauna, the library, the business alcove with its computer terminals and satellite phone—all the things that remind our passengers that they're never far from the comforts of home. These passengers can't understand that I prefer a sleeping bag on hard icy ground to soft sheets in a heated cabin. That I'd rather eat half-frozen food than a five-course meal. That I look forward to every moment away from the ship, when I hear the voices of penguins and petrels and feel farther than ever from the world above the sixtieth parallel.

WHEN I WAKE early the next morning, the other bunk in my cabin is empty. My roommate, Amy, must be up on deck, looking for albatross and petrels. Amy Lindstrom is the ship's undersea specialist, but she's just as fascinated with the creatures hovering above the water—and the Drake offers glimpses of birds we won't see farther south.

I should drag myself out of bed, too, but instead I prop myself up on one elbow and watch a wandering albatross just outside the porthole above my bunk. I'm always mesmerized by these birds who dominate the skies over the Southern Ocean; they spend months, sometimes years, at sea, circumnavigating this part of the planet without ever touching down on land. I observe the albatross for ten minutes, and he doesn't once flap his wings. He occasionally lets the wind lift him above the ship, out of my line of vision, but most of the time he glides a few inches over the waves, just out of reach of the roiling whitecaps.

I turn my head when I hear the door creak open, but I know it won't be the person I'd expected to see by now, the one I most want to see.

"Rise and shine," Thom says.

His tousled hair is spiked with more gray than I remember. I haven't seen Thom since we last camped out amid the penguins on Petermann Island five years ago, doing APP research, and yesterday, during the madness of getting passengers boarded and settled, we'd hardly had time to exchange more than a few words. Like most of the islands we'll visit with passengers over the next week, Petermann is inhabited only by Antarctic natives—birds and seals, lichens and mosses and algae, various invertebrates. Despite the long hours we put in there, counting penguins and crunching data, it's a quiet, peaceful existence. And now I know Thom and I will fall into the same rhythms, on land and on sea, alone or surrounded by tourists. We usually work in a companionable near silence, having learned each other's moods through weeks together at the bottom of the earth.

"Let me guess," I say. "Glenn sent you."

He nods. "It's showtime."

"What's next, costumes? Batons?"

"It's as good a time as any to make an appearance," Thom says. "It's a ghost ship right now. Last chance to eat a meal in relative quiet."

I sit up slowly, realizing by the steadiness of my stomach how much the waves have lessened, and while it's not exactly Drake Lake out there, I have no excuse to keep hiding down here.

I swing my legs over the side of the bunk. Because I shower at night and sleep in my clothes, I only have to pull back my hair before I'm ready to go.

I let Thom lead the way to the dining room and observe the slight limp with which he walks, the result of a fall into a crevasse on his first trip to Antarctica, more than a decade ago. Despite the swaying of the ship, despite my own need to let my hands trace the bulkhead for balance, he does not need to hold on to anything.

We sit down at an empty table with plates of toast and fruit, our full coffee mugs sloshing. The dining room is vacant except for a steward walking through with a tray, on his way to deliver nausea-calming ginger soup to one of the bedridden passengers.

"You're right," I say to Thom. "Gotta love a ghost ship."

He nods. I look at him for a moment, then ask about his kids, his wife, how it feels to be back. We usually don't spend a lot of time talking about our personal lives. But I have a question I need to ask him, and I want to ease into it.

After Thom fills me in on his wife's new job, his kids' transitions into the first and third grades, I bring it up. "So you were called in sort of last minute?"

He nods. "I contacted Glenn last year, thinking I'd be ready to come down again now that the kids are older. He said he didn't have any openings, but then he called a couple of months ago, asked me to fill in."

"For Keller?" I ask.

"Yeah."

"Did he tell you why?"

"I didn't ask." He looks at me. "You don't know?"

I shake my head. Out of the corner of my eye I glimpse a passenger entering the room, and I feel my shoulders shrink down, an automatic reflex, the instinct to hide. But the guy sees us and comes over, his plate piled high with eggs and sausage, which would turn my stomach even if we weren't rolling through the Drake. I know from the ship's doctor that about 60 percent of the men on board take heart medication. I also know that the second most requested pill on this ship, after meclizine for seasickness, is Viagra—and that the loss of blood flow to the right places is due more to artery-clogging food than to age.

And now this middle-aged guy, who actually looks trim and healthier than most, takes a seat across from Thom and me.

"Nice binocs," Thom comments, indicating the binoculars the man has placed on the table.

"Thanks," the man says, clearly pleased that Thom noticed. "Waterproof, shock resistant, image stabilizing. They've even got night vision."

"Not that you'll need it here," Thom says.

"What do you mean?"

"It doesn't get dark," Thom says. "Just a couple hours of dusk between sunset and sunrise."

The man looks out the nearest porthole, as if he's not sure whether to believe what he's heard. "Well, for what they cost me, I'll certainly use them for other trips after this," he says at last. "I'm Richard, by the way. Richard Archer."

"Thom Carson. And this is Deb Gardner. Welcome aboard." Thom rises to get more coffee, taking my mug with him.

I nod toward the binoculars. "May I?" I ask, reaching for them.

Richard pushes them across the spotless white tablecloth. "Be my guest."

I take the binoculars over to a porthole and raise them to my face. It takes me a moment to realize they're digital, that I have to press a button before my field of vision comes into sudden, sharp focus. Their power is incredible. After a few moments, I see the barnacle-encrusted gray head of a sperm whale, barely breaking the surface of the water as it refuels with air. I should announce this over the PA, but without binoculars like these, no one else is likely to see it.

I lower the binoculars and return to the table, handing them back.

"Maybe I did spend a little too much on them," Richard says, "but this is a once-in-a-lifetime trip, right? I don't want to miss anything."

"There's a sperm whale at eleven o'clock." I point toward the horizon and watch him scan for the whale. I imagine the tiny electronic pulses that are disassembling and reassembling reality at mind-boggling speed.

Thom returns, placing fresh coffee in front of me. "What do you see?" he asks Richard.

"I'm trying to find a sperm whale."

"It probably took a deep dive," I say. "Don't worry. You'll see others."

I'm not sure he will—typically only the males feed in this region, and they prefer the deepest of waters—but I try to be encouraging, to let people believe they're going to see everything possible, that they'll get their money's worth. They don't need to know that they could visit Antarctica every year for the rest of their lives and still not see all there is.

"So," Richard says, putting the binoculars back on the table, "how long have you worked on the *Cormorant*?"

"We're actually with the APP," Thom tells him.

"Oh?"

Thom's mouth is now full of toast, so I continue. "The Antarctic Penguins Project is a nonprofit organization," I explain. "We study the three species of penguins here, tracking their progress, numbers, feeding and breeding habits. The boat transports us down here as part of the project's mission to educate people about the region."

"Nice," Richard says. "If you have to be down here, this is the way to travel, that's for sure. What's our first stop?"

Thom explains that we won't know until just before we get there—that each excursion to these tiny, remote islands depends upon ice, weather, and access, all of which change day to day, sometimes hour to hour.

My mind wanders back a few days to when I arrived in

Ushuaia, at the guesthouse where Keller and I had planned to meet. He wasn't there, and I took the opportunity to shower off the long flight and to close my eyes for a little while. When I woke up, it was morning, and I was due at the dock where the *Cormorant* was moored—with still no sign of Keller.

I sent a quick e-mail from the computer in the hotel lobby, thinking his flight had been delayed and that he'd show up that evening, just before we cast off. But when the *Cormorant*'s long blast sounded and the ship drifted into the Beagle Channel, I looked past the passengers' faces, past their champagne glasses at the waters ahead, and I wanted, irrationally, to run up to the bridge, tell the captain we had to wait.

I stare out the view windows of the dining room and try to think optimistically: Keller must've missed his flight, shifted his schedule at the last minute, made a plan to join the *Cormorant* in Ushuaia on its next voyage south, two weeks from now. I tell myself this even as I doubt all of it. I sneak a glance at Richard, who is adjusting the settings on his binoculars, and in that moment we're not so different—both of us searching for something we aren't going to find.

The last time I said good-bye to Keller Sullivan was only three months earlier, during an unexpected Stateside visit. We still live on opposite coasts, and during the eight or more months we spend away from the continent, we keep in touch via e-mail, phone, and Skype. We're like penguins that way—each of us off on our own separate journeys until we meet again, our shared nests reserved for these expeditions, for the peninsula, for the camps we build together.

It's complicated, what we share—a relationship born among the penguins, among creatures whose own breeding habits are as ever-evolving as the oceans to which they're constantly struggling to adapt. While many species mate for life, others are monogamous for only one season; still others have surprisingly high divorce rates—for all of them, survival comes first. Sometimes I think this sums up Keller and me pretty well. We have fallen in love with each other as much as with Antarctica, and we have yet to separate ourselves, and what we are, from this place. Each time I arrive at the bottom of the world, I never quite know what our nest will look like, or if it'll exist at all.

Last season, when I arrived in Ushuaia, bleary-eyed and dreading our first week on the *Cormorant* before Keller and I would be dropped off at Petermann, I didn't see him until I was on board. Until I felt my duffel being lifted out of my hand, an arm around my waist. He spun me into a bear hug before I got a chance to look at him, then set me down so we could see each other.

"Here we are," he said. *"Fin del mundo—"*

"—principio de todo," I said, finishing the sentence for him as I usually did, repeating the town's motto, lettered in blue on the white wall that borders the colorful buildings of the town and the sharp, snowcapped mountains beyond them.

The end of the world, the beginning of everything.

Starting a journey to Antarctica doesn't feel right anymore without Keller. In a sudden flurry of emotions, I don't know which to give in to: worry, anger, or simply disappointment.

AS THE WAVES continue to lose their sting, guests begin to emerge from their cabins, unsteadily navigating the passageways. They don their waterproof, insulated, bright red *Cormorant* jackets and make their way topside.

The first few guests on the deck soon grow into a crowd of dozens, and it's not long before I'm surrounded, fielding their questions. *How fast do icebergs melt? Where will that one end up? How big do they get?*

"An iceberg the size of Singapore broke off a glacier not too long ago," I tell them. "But the largest one was even bigger than that, about two hundred miles long."

"Two hundred miles?" says the guy who'd asked. "That's like the distance from New York to D.C."

I nod but don't answer, never having been to either place. But I do understand their need to put their surroundings in context—I imagine I'd need to do the same if I were in New York or Washington. I'd need to compare the Washington Monument to the tallest pinnacle iceberg I'd seen, or compare the width of Times Square to one of the crevasses I'd come across on the continent.

But the truth is, right now I'm grateful for their questions. At least when they're talking I don't have to think about anything else, like where Keller is and why I haven't heard from him, or how I can possibly reach a man who rarely answers his cell phone and tends to stay offline for weeks at a time.

"Was that a penguin?" a man asks, blinking as if he's just seen a meteor.

I'd missed it, whatever he'd seen. "Could be," I tell him. "They feed in this area. Keep your eyes up ahead, off to the side of the boat, and you'll see them. The noise of the ship scares them out of the water."

I watch as the tourists lean over the railing; I listen to

rapid-fire sounds from their cameras. How quickly they duck behind their viewfinders—in their haste to capture images of the penguins, to gather their mementos, they miss the real beauty in everything there is to see. I have to remind myself of my own first journey south, when I took more photos than I could count, hardly daring to believe I'd have the chance to see any of it again. The penguins' sleek bodies porpoising through the waves, so fast they look like miniature orcas. The way they leap and swim in formation, as if they're in the sky instead of in the water. The way they change direction in the blink of an eye.

Gradually, the cold seeps in, and everyone shuffles inside. My shoulders begin to relax as I lean against the railing. It takes a moment before I realize I'm not alone.

A woman stands about twenty feet away, where the railing curves along the bow, and while she'd been facing the other direction, she's now turning toward me.

"Hi," she says and walks over. I see her glance at my name tag, and then she holds out her hand. "So you're the penguin expert," she says. "I'm Kate Archer."

After a brief pause, I take her hand, lost inside a puffed-up Gore-Tex glove. Her smile curves a half-moon into an otherwise lonely expression, and she seems so happy to meet me that I'm guessing she's traveling alone and hasn't talked to anyone in a while.

"This is amazing," she says. "I bet you never get sick of this view."

"No, I never do."

She points toward a berg in the distance. "How tall is that iceberg?"

"I'd say sixty, eighty feet." Then I add, "About the size of an eight-story building."

"Ah," she says, then falls back into silence.

I know I should be more friendly, engage her in conversation, educate her about the Antarctic, but I already feel as though I've used up my conversation quota for the day. And then I see something ahead—a flash of reflected light, indicating the presence of something I can't possibly be seeing.

I reach into my cargo pants and retrieve my binoculars, and I see I was right: In the distance is a ship, taller than the eight-story iceberg that is nearly hiding it.

I mutter, "What the hell?" and try to adjust my binoculars, wondering if they're fogged up, or broken—or if there's something wrong with my own eyes.

Then I glance over at the woman next to me, trying to remember her name. Kate. "Sorry," I say. "It's just that I can't believe what I'm seeing."

"What *are* you seeing?" She leans over the rail, as if that'll help her vision. "I don't know what you're talking about."

"You will," I say, lowering the binoculars. "Give it a second."

"I wish I had my husband's binoculars right now. I could probably see straight *through* that iceberg."

It takes me a second to make the connection. "Is your husband's name Richard?"

"Yes," she says, looking over at me. "Why?"

"I met him this morning. At breakfast."

"Then you've seen more of him today than I have."

There's something strange in her voice, but I'm not sure what it is. I've never been comfortable with the unnatural intimacy created on these voyages—we're witnesses to crumbling marriages, sibling rivalry, love affairs. Part of the problem, I think, is that, for so many, Antarctica is the trip of a lifetime, and their expectations are so high. They come down here expecting to be changed forever, and often they are, only not in the ways they expect. They get seasick, they aren't used to the close quarters, they learn that it's because of their own bad habits that the oceans are dying. And this all seeps into not only their dream vacation but their relationships, more deeply than they're prepared for.

Just then the ship begins to emerge from behind the iceberg, her bow nosing forward, revealing as she floats onward her many oversize parts: a vast, open-air terrace; a railing encompassing a sundeck and swimming pool; some sort of playing field just beyond. The ship comes slowly into full view, along with hundreds of tiny portholes and dozens of balconies feathered across the port side.

Even Kate looks surprised. "How far away is that boat?" she asks.

"Not far enough."

"It must be gigantic."

I nod. "Ten stories high, twelve hundred passengers, four hundred crew. And it has no business being down here."

"It looks like it made a wrong turn somewhere in the Caribbean. How do you know so much about it?"

"I've been studying the effects of tourism on the penguin colonies," I say. "I keep up on these things. The *Australis* is a new ship, registered in the Bahamas but probably filled with Americans—a floating theme park, like most of them."

"You're obviously not a fan."

"I have no problem with ships like this in the Caribbean or in Europe. But down here—the last thing any of us needs, least of all the penguins, is for that behemoth to dump a small town's worth of people on these islands."

"Then why is it allowed down here?"

I sigh, staring at the ship, which is moving along the horizon like a pockmarked iceberg. "No one owns these waters. They can do whatever they want."

"Is it headed south?"

"Looks like it," I say, then shrug. "The good news is that, most of the time, ships that big just dash across the Drake to give passengers a glimpse of the icebergs and then head back up north. So we probably won't see it again. It's way too big to get into most of the places we visit."

Kate's still looking at the cruise liner, and I'm heartened to see that she appears as disgusted by it as I am. "It makes even that iceberg look small."

I let out a wry laugh. "That iceberg is nothing compared to what we're getting into," I say. "And the *Australis* doesn't have a reinforced hull like we do. That's why I'm betting it will turn around."

"What if it does come across icebergs?" she asks. "How will it navigate around them?"

"Carefully," I tell her. "Very carefully."

FIVE YEARS BEFORE SHIPWRECK

Petermann Island

When I notice one of our gentoo chicks is missing, I flip through our field notebook, find the colony chart, and match nest to nest. According to our records, the chick was two weeks old, but now the rocky nest is empty. I search but find no body, which means its disappearance must have been the work of a predatory skua. When skuas swoop down to snatch chicks or eggs, they leave little behind.

I move away from the colony and sit on a rock to make some notes. That's when I hear it—a distinctly human yelp, and a thick noise that I have only heard once in my life and never forgotten: the sound of bone hitting something solid.

I stand up and see a man lying on the ground, a red-jacketed tourist from the *Cormorant*, which dropped its anchor in our bay this morning. The ship, making her rounds in the Antarctic peninsula, had left Thom and me here a week earlier, and she'll pick us up in another week, during the last cruise of the season.

Petermann Island is tiny, just over a mile long, once home

to small huts serving an early-twentieth-century French Antarctic expedition. Now we create our own research base, with tents and solar-powered laptops. During the two weeks we're here, the *Cormorant* stops by, weather permitting, to show tourists the birds and our camp, offering a tour of the island and a glimpse of how we researchers live.

The man had fallen hard, landing on his back. When I see a spot of red spreading from the rock under his head into the snow, I start toward him. Fifteen other tourists are within twenty yards, yet no one else seems to notice.

Thom must have seen something; he gets to the man first. And now a woman is scrambling guardedly down the same hill, apparently taking care, despite her hurry, to avoid the same fate.

I turn my attention to the man. His blood is an unwelcome sight, bright and thin amid the ubiquitous dark-pink guano of the penguins, and replete with bacteria, which could be deadly for the birds. I repress an urge to clean it up.

"Deb," Thom says sharply, glancing up. He'd spent two years in medical school before turning to marine biology, and he looks nervous. By now, four more tourists in their matching red jackets have gathered around us.

I hold out my arms and move forward, forcing the red jackets back a couple of steps. The woman who'd hurried down the hill is trying to see past me. She looks younger than the usual middle-aged passengers who cruise down to Antarctica. "Are you with him?" I ask her. "Where's your guide?"

"No—I don't know," she stammers. Blond hair trails from under her hat into her eyes, wide with an anxiety I can't place. "He's up there, maybe." She motions toward the gentoo colony. I glance up. The hill has nearly faded away in the fog.

"Someone needs to find him," I say. "And we need the doctor from the boat. Who's he traveling with?"

"His wife, I think," someone answers.

"Get her."

I kneel next to Thom, who's examining the man's head. If we were anywhere but Antarctica, the injury might not seem as critical. But we are at the bottom of the world, days away from the nearest city, even farther from the nearest trauma center. There's a doctor along on the cruise, and basic medical facilities at Palmer Station, a forty-person U.S. base an hour away by boat—but it's not yet clear whether that will be enough.

The man hasn't moved since he fell. A deep gash on the back of his head has bled through the thick wad of gauze Thom applied. Voices approach—the guide, the wife, the doctor. The man's chest suddenly begins to heave, and Thom quickly reaches out and turns his head so he can vomit into the snow.

The man shudders and tries to sit up, then loses consciousness again. Thom presses fresh gauze to his head and looks up.

"What happened?" the wife cries.

"He slipped," I tell her.

Susan Beecham, the ship's doctor, is now right behind us, and Thom and I move aside.

"How could this happen?" the wife wails.

I place a hand on her shoulder as crew members arrive with a gurney. "We need to get him to Palmer," Susan says, her voice low.

Thom helps them load him onto the gurney, and they take him to a Zodiac. I get a plastic bag from our camp, then return to the scene and begin scooping up the blood- and vomit-covered snow. Because this is one of the last pristine environments in the world, we go to great lengths to protect the animals from anything foreign. Visitors sterilize their boots before setting foot on the island, and again when they depart. No one leaves without everything they came with.

Yet sometimes, like now, it seems pointless. Injuries like this are unusual, but I've seen tourists drop used tissues and gum wrappers on the ground. I want to chase after them, to show them our data, to tell them how much the fate of the penguins has changed as more and more tourists pass through these islands. But I must be patient with this red-jacketed species. I'm grateful for the *Cormorant*'s transportation to this remote island, and the tour company's financial support of the APP, yet I often feel we earn it more each season, that our work takes a backseat to keeping the tourists happy.

Thom returns and stands over me. "They need me to go to Palmer with them."

I look up. "Why?"

"The crew is crazed," he says, "and they need someone to stay with the victim and his wife."

He doesn't have to explain; I can picture what's happening—Susan on the radio with the dispatcher at Palmer, deckhands preparing to pull anchor, naturalists answering worried passengers' questions, and Glenn trying to coordinate with the galley about the next meal and with the captain about the next destination.

"I guess we're at their mercy." I inspect the ground to make sure there's nothing left in the snow. Thom doesn't have a choice—we're often asked to fill in for the crew when we're on the island—but I know what he is really asking me. We've worked together for three years, and I've never spent a night here alone.

I stand up. Because Thom is short and I'm tall, we look each other directly in the eye. "Go ahead. I'll be all right."

"You sure?"

"I'll keep the radio on, just in case. But yeah, I'll be fine. After all this, I'll enjoy the peace."

"I'll be back tomorrow," he says.

We go back to camp, a trio of tents a few yards off the bay. From there we can watch the ships approach and, more important, depart.

Another Zodiac is waiting to take Thom to Palmer. He grabs a few things from his tent and gives my shoulder a squeeze before he leaves. "I'll buzz you later," he says. He smiles, and I feel a sudden, sharp loneliness, like an intake of cold air.

I watch the Zodiac retreat around the outer cliffs of the bay, then turn back to our empty camp.

ON AN EVENING like this, with the air sogged with unshed rain and the penguins splashing in a pool of slush nearby, it's hard to believe that Antarctica is the biggest desert in the world, the driest place on earth. The Dry Valleys have not seen rain for millions of years, and, thanks to the cold, nothing rots or decays. Even up here, on the peninsula, I've seen hundred-year-old seal carcasses in perfect condition, and abandoned whaling stations frozen in time. Those who perish in Antarctica—penguins, seals, explorers—are immortalized, the ice preserving life in the moment of death.

But for all that remains the same, Antarctica is constantly changing. Every year, the continent doubles in size as the ocean freezes around it; the ice shelf shifts; glaciers calve off. Whales once hunted are now protected; krill once ignored are now trawled; land once desolate now sees thousands of tourists a season.

I make myself a cold supper of leftover pasta and think of our return. Back on the *Cormorant,* Thom and I will be eating well, my solitude will be replaced with lectures and slide shows, and I'll wish I were here, among the penguins.

I finish eating and clean up. At nearly ten o'clock, it's bright outside, the sun still hours away from its temporary disappearance. I take a walk, heading up toward the colony that was so heavily trafficked today, the one the man visited before he fell. The penguins are still active, bringing rocks to fortify their nests, feeding their chicks. Some are sitting on eggs; others are returning from the sea to reunite with their mates, greeting one another with a call of recognition, a high-pitched rattling squawk.

I sit down on a rock, about fifteen feet away from the nearest nest, and watch the birds amble up the trail from the water. They appear to be ignoring me, but I know that they aren't; I know that their heart rates increase when I walk past, that they move faster when I'm around. Thom and I have been studying the two largest penguin colonies here, tracking their numbers and rates of reproduction, to gauge the effects of tourism and human contact. This island is one of the most frequently visited spots in Antarctica, and our data show that the birds have noticed: They're experiencing stress, lower birth rates, fewer fledging chicks. It's a strange irony that the hands that feed our research are the same hands that guide the *Cormorant* here every season, and I've often contemplated what will happen when the results of our study are published.

Sometimes when I watch the penguins, I become so mesmerized by the sounds of their purrs and squawks, by the precision of their clumsy waddle, that I forget I have another life, somewhere else—that I rent a cottage in Eugene, that I teach marine biology at the University of Oregon, that I'm thirty-four years old and not yet on a tenure track, that I haven't had a real date in three years. I forget that my life now is only as good as my next grant, and that when the money dries up, I'm afraid I will, too.

I first came to Antarctica eight years ago, to study the emperor penguins at McMurdo Station. I've returned every season since then, most frequently to these islands on the peninsula. It'll be years before our Antarctic Penguins Project study is complete, but because Thom's kids are young, he'll be taking the next few seasons off. I'm already looking forward to coming back next year.

What I'd like is to return to the Ross Sea, thousands of miles farther south, to the emperors—the only Antarctic birds that breed in winter, right on the ice. Emperors don't build nests; they live entirely on fast ice and in the water, never setting foot on solid land. I love that, during breeding season, the female lays her egg, scoots it over to the male, and then takes off, traveling a hundred miles across the frozen ocean to open water and swimming away to forage for food. She comes back when she's fat and ready to feed her chick.

My mother, who has given up on marriage and grandkids for her only daughter, says that this is my problem, that I think like an emperor. I expect a man to sit tight and wait patiently while I disappear across the ice. I don't build nests.

When the female emperor returns, she uses a signature call to find her partner. When they're reunited, they move in close and bob their heads toward each other, shoulder to shoulder in an armless hug, raising their beaks in what we call the ecstatic cry. Penguins are romantics. Many mate for life.

IN THE SUMMER, Antarctic sunsets last forever. The sky surrenders to an overnight dusk, a grayish light that dims around midnight. As I prepare to turn in, I hear the splatter of penguins bathing in their slush, the barely perceptible pats of their webbed feet on the rocks.

Inside my tent, I extinguish my lamp and set a flashlight nearby, turning over until I find a comfortable angle. The rocks are ice-cold, the padding under my sleeping bag far too thin. When I finally put my head down, I hear a loud splash— clearly made by something much larger than a penguin.

Feeling suddenly uneasy, I turn on my lamp again. I throw on a jacket, grab my flashlight, and hurry outside, climbing my way down to the rocky beach.

I can see a figure in the water, but it's bulky and oddly shaped, not smooth and sleek, like a seal. I shine my flashlight on it and see red.

It's a man, in his cruise-issued parka, submerged in the

water up to his waist. He looks into the glare of my flashlight. I stand there, too stunned to move.

The man turns away, and he takes another step into the water. *He's crazy*, I think. *Why would he go in deeper?* Sometimes the seasick medication that tourists take causes odd and even troubling behavior, but I've never witnessed anything like this.

As I watch him anxiously from the shore, I think of Ernest Shackleton. I think of his choices, the decisions he made to save the lives of his crew. His decision to abandon the *Endurance* in the Weddell Sea, to set out across the frozen water in search of land, to separate his crew from one another, to take a twenty-two-foot rescue boat across eight hundred miles of open sea—had any of these choices backfired, history would have an entirely different memory. In Antarctica, every decision is weighty, every outcome either a tragedy or a miracle.

Now, it seems, my own moment has come. It would be unthinkable to stand here and watch this man drown, but attempting a rescue could be even more dangerous. I'm alone. I'm wearing socks and a light jacket. The water is a few degrees above freezing, and, though I'm strong, this man is big enough to pull me under if he wanted to, or if he panicked.

Perhaps Shackleton only believed he had options. Here, genuine options are few.

I call out to the man, but my words dissolve in the foggy air. I walk toward him, into the bay, and my feet numb within seconds in the icy water. The man is now in up to his chest. By the time I reach him, he's nearly delirious, and he doesn't resist when I grab his arms, pull them over my shoulders, and steer us toward the shore. The water has nearly turned him into deadweight. Our progress is slow. Once on land, he's near collapse, and I can hardly walk myself. It takes all my strength to help him up the rocks and into Thom's tent.

He crumples on the tent floor, and I strip off his parka and his boots and socks. Water spills over Thom's sleeping bag and onto his books. "Take off your clothes," I say, turning away to rummage through Thom's things. I toss the man a pair of sweats, the only thing of Thom's that will stretch to fit his tall frame, and two pairs of thick socks. I also find a couple of T-shirts and an oversize sweater, and by the time I turn back to him, the man has put on the sweats and is feebly attempting the socks. His hands are shaking so badly he can hardly control them. Impatiently, I reach over to help, yanking the socks onto his feet.

"What the hell were you thinking?" I demand. I hardly look at him as I take off his shirt and help him squeeze into Thom's sweater. I turn on a battery-powered blanket and unzip Thom's sleeping bag. "Get in," I say. "You need to warm up."

His whole body shudders. He climbs in and pulls the blanket up to cover his shoulders.

"What are you doing here?" I, too, am shaking from the cold. "What the hell happened?"

He lifts his eyes, briefly. "The boat—it left me behind."

"That's impossible." I stare at him, but he won't look at me. "The *Cormorant* always does head counts. No one's ever been left behind."

He shrugs. "Until now."

I think about the chaos of earlier that day. It's conceivable that this stranger could have slipped through the cracks. And it would be just my luck.

"I'm calling Palmer. Someone will have to come out to take you back." I rise to my knees, eager to go first to my tent for dry clothes, then to the supply tent, where we keep the radio.

I feel his hand on my arm. "Do you have to do that just yet?" He smiles, awkwardly, his teeth knocking together. "It's just that—I've been here so long already, and I'm not ready to face the ship. It's embarrassing, to be honest with you."

"Don't you have someone who knows you're missing?" I regard him for the first time as a man rather than an alien in my world. His face is pale and clammy, its lines suggesting he is older than I am, perhaps in his mid-forties. I glance down to look for a wedding band, but his fingers are bare. Following my gaze, he tucks his hands under the blanket. Then he shakes his head. "I'm traveling alone."

"Have you taken any medication? For seasickness?"

"No," he says. "I don't get seasick."

"Well," I say, "we need to get someone out here to take you back to the *Cormorant*."

He looks at me directly for the first time. "Don't," he says.

I'm still kneeling on the floor of the tent. "What do you expect to do, stay here?" I ask. "You think no one will figure out you're missing?"

He doesn't answer. "Look," I tell him, "it was an accident. No one's going to blame you for getting left behind."

"It wasn't an accident," he says. "I saw that other guy fall. I watched everything. I knew that if I stayed they wouldn't notice me missing."

So he is crazy after all.

I stand up. "I'll be right back."

He reaches up and grasps my wrist so fast I don't have time

to pull away. I'm surprised by how quickly his strength has returned. I ease back down to my knees, and he loosens his grip. He looks at me through tired, heavy eyes—a silent plea. He's not scary, I realize then, but scared.

"In another month," I tell him, as gently as I can manage, "the ocean will freeze solid, and so will everything else, including you."

"What about you?"

"In a couple weeks, I'm leaving, too. Everyone leaves."

"Even the penguins?" The question, spoken through clattering teeth, lends him an innocence that almost makes me forgive his intrusions.

"Yes," I say. "Even they go north."

He doesn't respond. I stand up and head straight to the radio in our supply tent, hardly thinking about my wet clothes. Just as I'm contacting Palmer, I realize that I don't know the man's name. I go back and poke my head inside. "Dennis Marshall," he says.

The dispatcher at Palmer tells me that they'll pick Dennis up in the morning, when they bring Thom back. "Unless it's an emergency," he says. "Everything okay?"

I want to tell him it's not okay, that this man could be crazy, dangerous, sick. Instead I pause, then say, "We're fine. Tell Thom we'll see him in the morning."

I return to the tent. Dennis has not moved.

"What were you doing in the water?" I ask.

"Thought I'd try to catch up to the boat," he says.

"Very funny. I'm serious."

He doesn't reply. A moment later, he asks, "What are *you* doing here?"

"Research, obviously."

"I know," he says. "But why come here, to the end of the earth?"

It's always been hard to explain why a place like Antarctica is perfect for me. Before you can sign on to overwinter at McMurdo, they give you psych tests to make sure you can live for months in darkness and near isolation without going crazy—and the idea of this has always amused me. It's not the isolation that threatens to drive me insane; it's civilization.

"What kind of question is that?" I ask Dennis.

"You know what I mean," he says. "You have to be a real loner to enjoy being down here." He rubs the fingers of his left hand.

I catch his hand to examine his fingers. "Where do they hurt?"

"It's not that," he says.

"Then what?"

He hesitates. "I dropped my ring," he says. "My wedding band."

"Where? In the water?"

He nods.

"For God's sake." I duck out of the tent before he can stop me. I hear his voice behind me, asking me where I'm going, and I shout back, "Stay there."

I rush toward the water's edge, shivering in my still-damp clothes. The penguins purr as I go past, and a few of them scatter. I shine my flashlight down through the calm, clear water to the rocks at the bottom. I don't know where he might have dropped the ring, so I wade in, and within minutes my feet feel like blocks of ice. I follow what I think was his path into the water, sweeping the flashlight back and forth in front of me.

I'm in up to my knees when I see it, a few feet down—a flash of gold against the slate-colored rocks. I reach in, the water up to my shoulder, so cold it feels as if my arm will snap off and sink.

I manage to grasp the ring with fingers that now barely move, then shuffle back to shore on leaden feet. I hobble back to my own tent, where I strip off my clothes and don as many dry things as I can. My skin is moist and wrinkled from being wet for so long. I hear a noise and look up to see Dennis, blanket still wrapped around his shoulders, crouched at the opening to my tent.

"What are you staring at?" I snap. Then I look down to what he sees—a thin, faded T-shirt, no bra, my nipples pressing against the fabric, my arm flushed red from the cold. I pull his ring off my thumb, where I'd put it so it wouldn't fall again, and throw it at him.

He picks it up off the floor. He holds it but doesn't put it on. "I wish you'd just left it," he says, almost to himself.

"A penguin could have choked on it," I say. "But no one ever thinks about that. We're all tourists here, you know. This is their home, not ours."

"I'm sorry," he says. "What can I do?"

I shake my head.

He comes in and sits down, then pulls the blanket off his shoulders and places it around mine. He finds a fleece pullover in a pile of clothing and wraps it around my reddened arm.

"How cold is that water, anyway?" he asks.

"About thirty degrees, give or take." I watch him carefully.

"How long can someone survive in there?"

"A matter of minutes, usually," I say, remembering an expedition guide who'd drowned. He'd been trapped under his flipped Zodiac for only a few moments but had lost consciousness, with rescuers only a hundred yards away. "Most people go into shock. It's too cold to swim, even to breathe."

He unwraps my arm. "Does it feel better?"

"A little." Pain prickles my skin from the inside, somewhere deep down, and I feel an ache stemming from my bones. "You still haven't told me what you were doing out there."

He reaches over and begins massaging my arm. I'm not sure I want him to, but I know the warmth, the circulation, is good. "Like I said, I lost my ring."

"You were out much farther than where I found your ring."

"I must have missed it." He doesn't look at me as he speaks. I watch his fingers on my arm, and I am reminded of the night before, when only Thom and I were here, and Thom had helped me wash my hair. The feel of his hands on my scalp, on my neck, had run through my entire body, tightening into a coil of desire that never fully vanished. But nothing has ever happened between Thom and me, other than unconsummated rituals: As we approach the end of our stays, we begin doing things for each other—he'll braid my long hair; I'll rub his feet—because after a while touch becomes necessary.

I pull away. I regard the stranger in my tent: his dark hair, streaked with silver; his sad, heavy eyes; his ringless hands, still outstretched.

"What's the matter?" he asks.

"Nothing."

"I was just trying to help." The tent's small lamp casts deep shadows under his eyes. "I'm sorry," he says. "I know you don't want me here."

Something in his voice softens the knot in my chest. I sigh. "I'm just not a people person, that's all."

For the first time, he smiles, barely. "I can see why you come here. Talk about getting away from it all."

"At least I leave when I'm supposed to," I say, offering a tiny smile of my own.

He glances down at Thom's clothing, pulled tight across his body. "So when do I have to leave?" he asks.

"They'll be here in the morning."

Then he says, "How's he doing? The guy who fell?"

It takes me a moment to realize what he's talking about. "I don't know," I confess. "I forgot to ask."

He leans forward, then whispers, "I know something about him."

"What's that?"

"He was messing around with that blond woman," he says. "The one who was right there when it happened. I saw you talking to her."

"How do you know?"

"I saw them. They had a rendezvous every night, on the deck, after his wife went to bed. The blonde was traveling with her sister. They even ate lunch together once, the four of them. The wife had no idea."

"Do you think they planned it?" I ask. "Or did they just meet on the boat?"

"I don't know."

I look away, disappointed. "She seemed too young. For him."

36

"You didn't see her hands," he says. "My wife taught me that. You always know a woman's age by her hands. She may have had the face of a thirty-five-year-old, but she had the hands of a sixty-year-old."

"If you're married, why are you traveling alone?"

He pauses. "Long story."

"Well, we've got all night," I say.

"She decided not to come," he says.

"Why?"

"She left, a month ago. She's living with someone else."

"Oh." I don't know what more to say. Dennis is quiet, and I make another trip to the supply tent, returning with a six-pack of beer. His tired eyes brighten a bit.

He drinks before speaking again. "She was seeing him for a long time," he says, "but I think it was this trip that set her off. She didn't want to spend three weeks on a boat with me. Or without him."

"I'm sorry." A moment later, I ask, "Do you have kids?"

He nods. "Twin girls, in college. They don't call home much. I don't know if she's told them or not."

"Why did you decide to come anyway?"

"This trip was for our anniversary." He turns his head and gives me a cheerless half smile. "Pathetic, isn't it?"

I roll my beer can between my hands. "How did you lose the ring?"

"The ring?" He looks startled. "It fell off during the land-ing, I guess."

"It was thirty degrees today. Weren't you wearing gloves?"

"I guess I wasn't."

I look at him, knowing there is more to the story and that

neither of us wants to acknowledge it. And then he lowers his gaze to my arm. "How does it feel?" he asks.

"It's okay."

"Let me work on it some more." He begins to rub my arm again. This time he slips his fingers inside the long sleeve of my shirt, and the sudden heat on my skin seems to heighten my other senses: I hear the murmur of the penguins, feel the wind rippling the tent. At the same time, it's all drowned out by the feel of his hands.

I lean back and pull him with me until his head hovers just above mine. The lines sculpting his face look deeper in the tent's shadowy light, and his lazy eyelids lift as if to see me more clearly. He blinks, slowly, languidly, as I imagine he might touch me, and in the next moment he does.

I hear a pair of gentoos reunite outside, their rattling voices rising above the night's ambient sound. Inside, Dennis and I move under and around our clothing, our own voices muted, whispered, breathless, and in the sudden humid heat of the tent we've recognized each other in the same way, by instinct, and, as with the birds, it's all we know.

DURING THE ANTARCTIC night, tens of thousands of male emperors huddle together through months of total darkness, in temperatures reaching seventy degrees below zero, as they incubate their eggs. By the time the females return to the colony, four months after they left, the males have lost half their body weight and are near starvation. Yet they wait. It's what they're programmed to do.

Dennis does not wait for me. I wake up alone in my tent, the gray light of dawn nudging my eyelids. When I look at my watch, I see that it's later than I thought.

Outside, I glance around for Dennis, but he's not in camp. I make coffee, washing Thom's cup for him to use. I drink my own coffee without waiting for him; it's the only thing to warm me this morning, with him gone and the sun so well hidden.

I sip slowly, steam rising from my cup, and take in the moonscape around me: the edgy rocks, the mirrored water, ice sculptures rising above the pack ice—I could be on another planet. Yet for the first time in years, I feel as if I've reconnected with the world in some way, as if I am not as lost as I've believed all this time.

I hear the sound of a distant motor and stand up. Then it stops. I listen, hearing agitated voices—it must be Thom, coming from Palmer, having engine trouble. He is still outside the bay, out of sight, so I wait, rinsing my coffee mug and straightening up. When the engine starts up again, I turn back toward the bay. A few minutes later, Thom comes up from the beach with one of the electricians at Palmer, a young guy named Andy. I wave them over.

They walk hesitantly, and when they get closer, I recognize the look on Thom's face, and I know, with an icy certainty, where Dennis is, even before Thom opens his mouth.

"We found a body, Deb," he says. "In the bay." He exchanges a glance with Andy. "We just pulled him in."

I stare at their questioning faces. "He was here all night," I say. "I thought he just went for a walk, or—" I stop. Then I start toward the bay.

Thom steps in front of me. He holds both of my arms. "There's no need to do this," he says.

But I have to see for myself. I pull away and run to the beach. The body lies across the rocks. I recognize Thom's sweater, stretched across Dennis's large frame.

I walk over to him; I want to take his pulse, to feel his heartbeat. But then I see his face, a bluish white, frozen in an expression I don't recognize, and I can't go any closer.

I feel Thom come up behind me. "It's him," I say. "I gave him your sweater."

He puts an arm around my shoulder. "What do you think happened?" he asks, but he knows as well as I do. There is no current here, no way to be swept off this beach and pulled out to sea. The Southern Ocean is not violent here, but it is merciless nonetheless.

ANTARCTICA IS NOT a country; it is governed by an international treaty whose rules apply almost solely to the environment. There are no police here, no firefighters, no medical examiners. We have to do everything ourselves, and I shrug Thom off when he tries to absolve me from our duties. I help them lift Dennis into the Zodiac, the weight of his body entirely different now. I keep a hand on his chest as we back out of the bay and speed away, as if he might suddenly try to sit up. When we arrive at Palmer, I finally give in, leaving him to the care of others, who will pack his body for the long journey home.

They offer me a hot shower and a meal. As Andy walks me

down the hall toward the dormitory, he tries in vain to find something to say. I'm silent, not helping him. Eventually he updates me on the injured man. "He's going to be okay," he tells me. "But you know what's strange? He doesn't remember anything about the trip. He knows his wife, knows who the president is, how to add two and two—but he doesn't know how he got here, or why he even came to Antarctica. Pretty spooky, huh?"

He won't remember the woman he was fooling around with, I think. *She will remember him, but for him, she's already gone.*

BACK AT CAMP, I watch for the gentoos who lost their chick, but they do not return. Their nest remains abandoned, and other penguins steal their rocks.

Thom makes a few attempts to ask about Dennis, and when I meet his questions with silence, he stops asking. We both know what lies ahead—an investigation, paperwork, corporate lawyers, questions from the family—and I don't want to go through it any more than I need to.

Six days later, Thom and I break camp and ready ourselves for the weeklong journey back. Once we are on the boat, the distractions are plenty, and the hours and days fly past in seminars and lectures. The next thing I know, we are a day away from the Drake Passage.

I wander around the ship, walking the passageways Dennis walked, sitting where he must have sat, standing where he may have stood. I'm with a new group of passengers now, none of whom would have crossed his path. A sleety rain begins to fall, and I go out to the uppermost deck, the small one reserved for crew. As we float through a labyrinth of icebergs, I play with Dennis's wedding ring, which he'd left on the floor of my tent. I wear it on my thumb, as I did when I'd first found it, because that's where it fits.

It's probably because of this vantage point that I see her— an emperor penguin in the distance, standing alone atop an enormous tabular iceberg. It's uncommon to see an emperor this far north, and a good field guide would announce the sighting on the PA—the passengers aren't likely to get another chance to see an emperor.

But I don't move. I watch her as she preens her feathers, as she senses the sounds and vibrations of our ship and raises her head—an elegant, gentle pirouette in our direction. It feels as though she's looking directly at me, and in that moment we are mirror images of each other, lone figures above the vastness of all this sea and ice. She's so far from her breeding grounds that for a moment I wonder whether she's lost, but when she looks away and turns back to her feathers, I sense instead that she is feeling leisurely, safe, enjoying a rare moment of peace before returning home.

ONE WEEK BEFORE SHIPWRECK

The Drake Passage
(59°39'S, 61°56'W)

Thom and I stand together on the rear deck, watching the *Australis* moving in the distance like a time-lapse image of a drifting iceberg: slow, massive, inevitable. In one of the articles I'd read about the ship, a spokesman for the parent cruise company had bragged about how the *Australis* would cruise to every last inch of the planet, that no place was off-limits to a ship this invincible. It reminded me of what people once said about the *Titanic*.

The last disaster down here happened a few years ago, when a small tourist ship sank fourteen hours after colliding with an iceberg. That ship was lucky enough to be within an hour of another boat, and small enough that all her passengers could be rescued — but of course thousands of gallons of fuel were spilled, coating the penguins, destroying their waterproof feathers.

I tighten my grip on the railing. "It just drives me insane to see that ship down here. Maybe Glenn can nail them on some IAATO violation or something."

"I doubt it," Thom says.

I sigh. "What good is an association that's supposed to protect this place from cruise ships if membership is voluntary?"

Thom doesn't answer; this conundrum frustrates us all. Back in the early nineties, when the International Association of Antarctica Tour Operators was founded, only six thousand travelers a year visited Antarctica—now it's closer to forty thousand. That alone makes our instincts to protect the continent seem futile—not to mention the fact that there's no such thing as an Antarctic coast guard.

And nothing yet has prevented the cruise-bys: the ships that come down just so their passengers can say they've been. I'd complained about it to Keller the last time I saw him, which wasn't long after I'd read yet another story about the fancy new *Australis*. He'd tried to make the point that our *Cormorant* passengers are no different—they are simply able to pay more for the luxury of a small expedition with scientists and Antarctic experts on board, and all passengers sign liability waivers no matter what ship they're on. We'd argued about it, but in a way, of course, he's right. We're all at risk down here because every day we venture into the unknown.

Thom pushes away from the railing. "I'll go up to the bridge," he says. "See what I can find out."

I nod. A nausea spreads through me that is far worse than seasickness, far worse than the guilt of taking our own hundred tourists to shore. Down here, ships look after one another—but how do you look after a ship that's more than ten times the size of your own?

Thom doesn't return, and after a while I assume he's been detained by a tourist or given a task. I step inside, to the lounge, where small groups of passengers gather around tables drinking coffee; a few sit alone in chairs, reading or gazing out the view windows. My roommate, Amy, is setting up the afternoon slide show. As a full-time employee of the tour company, Amy travels from Antarctica to Alaska, from Mexico to the Galápagos, and she's often with the *Cormorant* during the entire Antarctic season, late November through early February. This is her fifth year in Antarctica, and we always bunk together when we can.

"What're you showing later?" I ask.

"Just some footage from the ROV," she says.

The ship's remotely operated vehicle reaches depths of up to a thousand feet, far deeper than Amy herself can dive—and her video of the ocean floor is alive with colorful and intricate corals, ghostly icefish, pale sea sponges, graceful brittle stars.

"Any footage of the yeti crab yet?" The existence of a blind, hairy Antarctic yeti crab is a new discovery, first seen in the Southern Ocean just a few years ago, and I'm always teasing Amy because it drives her crazy that she hasn't captured it on film yet. Last season, Keller helped me Photoshop images of the elusive crab into places on board the *Cormorant*— on a table in the dining room, next to a glass of beer in the lounge—and throughout the voyage we'd e-mail them to Amy, writing, *Did you see the yeti crab?*

"Piss off," Amy says cheerfully as she taps at her laptop's keyboard. She leans over to attach the laptop to the projector, then accidentally tangles the cord around her arm and pulls the projector off the table. She catches it just before it hits the floor.

Amy is small, with a soft, pale beauty, as if she herself had emerged from the unblemished depths of the sea, and when she puts on a dry suit and scuba gear and descends into the water, she disappears below the surface seamlessly, as if she belongs there. When she's not under the water or on board a cruise vessel, she writes picture books for kids.

A blast of cold air comes through the lounge, and I turn to see Kate and Richard Archer walk in. I let my eyes linger on them, curious. Kate's hair is windblown, curling into ringlets from the moist air outside, and her skin is flushed with cold. She stands close to Richard; he's more than a head taller, with wheat-colored hair and a thin build. As they walk toward a table, I realize from his slower gait that he's at least ten years older than she is. After they sit down, he looks at Kate, then reaches out and tucks a lock of hair behind her ear. Her round face breaks into a smile as the curl bounces loose, back into her face, and then she leans forward and gives him a kiss.

"So where's Keller?"

I turn back to Amy and shrug.

"I thought he'd be here," she says.

"So did I."

"So what happened?"

"Wish I knew."

Amy is looking over my shoulder. "Well, there's Glenn," she says. "Ask him."

Glenn is talking to the bartender, and I walk over, standing a bit behind him until they finish.

"Hey, Glenn," I say as he turns around. "Do you have a second?"

Glenn looks at me, waiting. He has a smooth, unblemished face partially hidden by a perfectly trimmed goatee. His physical youthfulness is belied by a consistently somber expression and dark, serious eyes. I try to remember the last time I saw him smile, and I can't.

"I wanted to ask you about Keller."

"What about him?"

"Why isn't he on board?"

"He didn't tell you?"

I feel my face redden. "If I knew, I wouldn't be asking you."

"Deb, I'm not sure I should be talking about this. It's technically a human resources issue."

"Really?" I say. "You're going to hide behind human resources?"

Glenn sighs. "You remember that last voyage," he says. "It shouldn't come as any surprise that Keller is no longer welcome on this ship."

I shouldn't be surprised—but I am. While I knew Keller had pushed Glenn's limits, neither of them had given me any indication that Keller wouldn't be here when the season began.

"Why didn't you talk to me?" I say. "I would have vouched for him. Kept an eye on him."

"This isn't child care, Deb. And clearly he didn't want you to know." I sense that Glenn is censoring a snide remark. "He came to see me in Seattle. He lobbied hard to come back, I'll give him that."

I'd nearly forgotten about Keller's quick trip from Eugene to Seattle. About a job, he'd said. But he'd never mentioned Glenn.

"I did consider it," Glenn continues, "for the sake of the APP and the fact that he's a good worker. But I can't take any more drama."

"He was only telling the truth."

"People come on this trip to be entertained," Glenn says, "not accused."

"They also come to be educated. What about awareness? Isn't that part of it?"

"You know as well as I do that you can't raise awareness if you don't have any passengers," Glenn says. "And those who do come here—well, they deserve better."

"It was that one guy who started it," I say. "I remember—"

"That passenger," Glenn interrupts, "demanded a full refund, or he threatened to sue. I can't afford to employ Keller. Simple as that."

I try to process what this means.

"So I take it he didn't tell you where he is now?" Glenn says.

I look at him, waiting.

"He's on the *Australis*."

"What? That's impossible."

"He asked me for a reference," Glenn says. "Wisely, it was for a position with minimal passenger interaction. I just spoke to the HR manager last week."

"But he would never—" I stop, the nausea I'd felt earlier suddenly surging back.

"Are you okay?"

"I'm fine."

Glenn looks as though he's about to say something more, but the nausea overtakes me, and I push past him to the nearest lavatory. I lean over the toilet, and even as I tell myself it's just seasickness, maybe a minor stomach bug, I can't help but remember the last time I'd felt this way, years ago, after Dennis—the caustic feeling of having been left out, left behind.

McMurdo Station

McMurdo Station is a U.S. base on Ross Island, on the south side of the Antarctic continent and in the shadow of Mt. Erebus. The planes used to transport scientists and staff from Christchurch, New Zealand, are like large tin cans with rows of military-grade seating, cramped and cold. At this time of year, during the austral summer, when McMurdo is the Grand Central Station of Antarctica, with its maximum capacity of twelve hundred residents, the planes are as packed as commercial jets during the holidays.

I secure my bag in the middle of the fuselage, take a seat, and close my eyes for the eight-hour flight. I'm heading to McMurdo on a National Science Foundation grant to do a census of the emperor colony nearest the base. During the station's busiest period, the LC-130 cargo planes arrive regularly to bring people and supplies. Eventually the flights will taper off, and from February to October, except for the very rare fly-in, planes won't land at McMurdo at all.

I hear a voice above me. "Seat taken?"

I open my eyes and say, "Suit yourself." A guy about my age is pulling down the metal bar of the jump seat next to mine. He's tall and thin, with overgrown dark hair that falls into his eyes and a red bandanna loose around his neck.

The guy leans his head back against the red nylon webbing that constitutes our seats, his head angled toward mine. "It's my first time here," he says.

"Mmm."

"And you? You look like an old-timer."

I look over at him.

"I don't mean *old*," he says. "Just—experienced. Like you know the drill."

"Yeah, I get it. You here to do research?"

"To do dishes, actually," he says. "I'm with maintenance. Just something to get me down here. What about you?"

"I'm studying the emperors at Garrard."

He regards me with new interest. "Really? Is that the colony that was wrecked by that iceberg?"

I'm surprised, and pleased, that he knows of the colony; so many who come to McMurdo for the manual labor and maintenance jobs seem to know about the wildlife only on a superficial level.

"I'm Keller," he offers. "Keller Sullivan."

"I'm Deb."

"Good to meet you," he says.

"Likewise."

"I'd love to hear more about the colony," he says.

He's turned his head and is looking at me almost sideways. In the dim industrial lighting, the dark of his eyes deepens against his pale face.

"Maybe later? I'm a little tired," I say. "Didn't sleep at all on the flight to Christchurch."

"Me, neither," he says.

I let my eyes fall shut again. It's not often anymore that my mind wanders toward Dennis, but right now, it goes straight back. I'm always surprised by how, even after all this time, it can feel like only days ago.

There'd been an investigation, of course, an autopsy, more questions than I knew how to handle. The worst was the media. News of the investigation had leaked out—everything from the fact that Dennis and I had spent the night together to details on his drowning. I think the family hoped, and I certainly did, that Dennis's death would've been kept as private as possible—but when something happens in Antarctica, it's newsworthy by default. Everyone knew, from my colleagues at the university to the tourists on the new season's trips south. The investigation ruled Dennis's death a suicide; the tour company and everyone involved, including me, were officially off the hook.

I still have his ring, the wedding band he'd tried so hard to lose. I've kept it hidden away in a small box at the top of my closet with a few other valuables. No one had ever asked about it. When I saw pictures of his wife in the news, I convinced myself that, by being there with him during his last hours, I had more right to keep it than she ever would, since she'd been off with someone else when he died.

I drift away to sleep, and the next thing I know, I'm awakened by an announcement from the pilot. I open my eyes and see Keller's confused face. When I hear the sighs and groans of everyone in the cabin, I know what the news is—the plane is turning around.

"What's a boomerang?" Keller asks.

"Bad weather at the station," I explain. "If the plane can't land at McMurdo, the pilot has to turn around."

He nods. We don't speak again, and we go our separate ways when we land back in Christchurch. When I arrive at the Antarctic Program passenger terminal the next day, I don't see him. But then, soon after I board, I feel someone sink into the seat next to mine, and there he is.

"We meet again," he says.

All around us, passengers are pulling their parka hoods over their heads and faces, preparing to sleep, and I offer Keller a brief smile and then do the same, closing my eyes quickly so I don't have to look at him, so he won't keep talking to me.

The only problem is, I can see his face even with my eyes closed.

I remain awake, aware of Keller beside me, of his arm lightly brushing mine as he reaches into one of his bags, as he opens a book to read. I don't know how much time passes until I feel movement next to me again, what I think is the motion of Keller leaning his head back against the netting behind us.

Finally I succumb to sleep—there is little else to do on these flights—and wake to a dull pain in my neck. I've slouched over in my seat, my head resting on Keller's shoulder.

I straighten up, mumbling an apology. Then I notice that he looks very pale. The LC-130 is heaving and pitching in the sky. "I don't remember it being this bad the last time," he says.

"We didn't make it this far last time. It's often like this when we get close."

I watch his face, just a hint of tension under the stubble of his jaw, and when he gives me a sheepish grin, I notice that his brown eyes are streaked through with a color that reminds me of the algae veining the snow on the peninsula islands—a muted, cloudy green.

There are no armrests on an LC-130, nowhere to put your hands during a stressful landing. Keller is gripping his knees, his knuckles white. Biting back a smile, I reach over to pat his hand in a *there, there* sort of gesture, and I'm surprised when he turns his palm upward to clasp mine.

There's not really any such thing as a routine landing at McMurdo, and by the time we approach the ice-hardened runway, the storm has whipped up whiteout conditions. The pilot circles several times in an attempt to wait out the weather, but eventually he must descend. When the plane touches its skis down on the ice, a sudden gust of wind seems to take hold of its tail, spinning it across the runway and nose-first into a fresh bank of snow.

But the plane holds together, as do Keller and I, our hands still clasped. After the plane stops moving, we let go at the same time. I try to ignore the fact that I hadn't been ready to let go. That a man's hand in mine, after so long, had felt good.

With Keller behind me, I step through the hatch, down the half dozen steps to the ice. The air hitting my face is so cold it stings, the whirling snow a blinding white. As I put my hand up to shield my eyes, I see the Terra Bus that will transport us to the station from the runway. The bus is even more cramped than the plane, and after boarding I don't see Keller among the parkas, hats, and luggage stuffed inside. Fifteen minutes later, the station comes into view through the bus's small, square windows.

With its bare industrial buildings, McMurdo looks like an ugly desert town whose landscape is drab and brown at the height of the austral summer and so white in the winter that you don't know which way is up. On clear days, Mt. Erebus is visible in the distance, steam rising from its volcanic top, and later in the season, when the sun finally begins to set, the mountain looks as if it's on fire.

I'm stretching my legs, taking it all in, when I notice Keller watching me.

"I was thinking," he says. "Maybe I could shadow you out there one day? See the colony firsthand."

I tell him, "Maybe," both charmed by his interest and a bit wary of it.

We've been assigned to different dorms and say quick good-byes before going our separate ways. We don't make plans to see each other, but I know I'll eventually bump into him around the station, in the cafeteria. At McMurdo, during the busy season, you can't avoid people even if you want to.

Yet I don't see him again until two days later, when I'm heading out for my fieldwork and find him standing outside the Mechanical Equipment Center, wearing a jacket that looks too light for the temperature and that same red bandanna tied around his neck like a scarf.

"Hey," Keller says in greeting as I approach the building. "Are you heading to the Garrard colony?"

"That's right."

"Is this a good time for me to tag along?" he asks.

I look at him, wondering how serious he really is about learning about the penguins. "Don't you have dishes to wash?"

"Not until tonight," he says.

"Why don't you spend some time getting the lay of the land?" I suggest. "You could visit Scott's hut—it's a nice walk from here."

"Already tried," he says. "It's closed for renovations. Indefinitely, they told me. What are they doing in there, anyway? Adding indoor plumbing? Central heating?"

I can't help but smile.

"I promise I won't get in your way," he says.

I glance toward the MEC building, then back at Keller. "Have you been trained on the snowmobiles?"

He shakes his head. "Not yet."

Which means if he comes along, he'll need to ride with me. There's just enough room for two on the Ski-Doo, and I don't carry many supplies for day trips: a counter, field notebook, water, pee bottle and plastic bags, and a survival kit, all tucked into a compartment of the snowmobile.

"I'm not on a schedule," I warn him. "I can't drive you all the way back here so you can be on time for your shift."

He grins. "You scientists. No respect for the workingman."

I give him a look, but he's still smiling. "What're they going to do, fire me?"

"Probably."

He only shrugs. "Look, I may not know a lot about penguins yet," he says, "but I could be a great assistant."

I'm not sure I need an assistant, but I consider it anyway. There's a lot of data to collect, and he could be helpful—as long as I don't have to spend my time picking up after him or fixing his mistakes. At least he knows about the colony, which is something. A decade earlier, a gigantic iceberg calved off the Ross Ice Shelf and blocked the penguins' access to the ocean, their only source of food. They had to find a new path, which was more than twice as long. None of the chicks survived that season, and most of the adults starved. Once a fairly healthy colony, with thousands of breeding pairs, it had to start over—but it's been recovering, growing slowly, and thanks to our five-year grant from the NSF, someone from the Antarctic Penguins Project travels down here to do the annual census. This year, it's me.

"I guess I could use an extra hand," I say. Keller's smile is so genuine I can't resist smiling back.

It's a clear day, with lucent vanilla ice sandwiched between blue ocean and bluer sky. When we arrive at the colony, I set about my work, instructing Keller to either stay put and watch or follow my footsteps exactly so as not to disturb the molting birds.

"It's called a catastrophic molt for a reason," I tell him. Unlike most other birds, penguins molt their feathers all at once, rather than shed them gradually. The emperors' molt happens over a month, a physically exhausting feat that uses up all their energy. The penguins, fattened up in preparation, look as though they've gotten bad haircuts, their brownish feathers sloughing off in a patchwork of fluff, the beautiful, sleek new feathers coming in underneath.

"Don't do anything to cause them to move," I say. "They need every bit of energy they've got."

Keller nods and follows me, just as slowly and carefully as I've instructed. In addition to counting the birds—a job made easier by the fact that they're molting and standing still—I slip quietly among them to inspect carcasses on the ground. The dead are mostly chicks, killed by starvation or skuas—the mean-beaked predators that feed off penguin eggs and dead chicks—but this means that at least the adults are making it back out to the ocean to feed.

It isn't until later that afternoon, when I press my hand into an ache in my back, that Keller suggests we take a break. "You haven't stopped once," he says.

I look at my watch—it's been five hours since we left the station. And it occurs to me that Keller hasn't stopped either; he hasn't gotten cold or tired or hungry.

"I always lose track of time out here," I say, almost to myself.

He swings his slim backpack off his shoulder. "I brought lunch."

"You go ahead," I say.

"You forgot to bring food, didn't you?"

"I don't usually eat when I'm in the field."

"I have enough for both of us," he says. "Sit down."

He shakes out a small, waterproof blanket, and we settle down about thirty yards away from the birds. I don't bother looking at Keller's food—vegans become accustomed to not sharing meals. It can be rare even to meet garden-variety vegetarians down here.

But Keller's pack is filled with fruit and bread, with containers of leftover rice and beans and salad. "Seriously?" I ask.

"Rabbit food, I know," he says, as if he's had to defend his food a hundred times before. "It's all I've got. Take it or leave it."

I almost laugh with the sudden pleasure of this strange, simple thing—sitting with Keller on the ice, sharing a meal among the molting emperors, on a blindingly bright Antarctic day. It's been so long since I've made a connection with someone else. I haven't been with anyone since Dennis, and even after a year, it hasn't been difficult; in fact, life's been a lot simpler. Or maybe I've just managed to convince myself of that.

In science, in the natural world, things make sense. Animals act on instinct—of course, they have emotions, personalities; they can be cheeky or manipulative or surprising—but, unlike humans, they don't cause intentional harm. Humans are a whole different story, and I learned at a young age that, in most people, meanness is more instinctual than kindness. I'd been a boyish kid—tall for my age, with cropped blond hair, a science geek. After being physically kicked out of the girls' restroom in junior high by girls who were convinced I was a boy, I grew my hair halfway down my back. I wore it that long, usually braided, until just last year, when I chopped it to right below my chin—long enough to look like a female, since I never wear makeup, and to still be able to pull it back and out of the way.

"What is it?" Keller asks. "What're you thinking about?"

"Nothing," I say, and he hands me a fork.

"How long have you been with the APP?" he asks.

"About eight, nine years." I take a bite of salad and rice. "And what about you? What did you do before entering the world of janitorial services?"

He shrugs. "Something a lot less interesting."

There's something closed off about the way he speaks, and I don't ask him anything else. We finish eating, and I get back to work. Despite my earlier vow not to cater to Keller's schedule, I get everything loaded back into the snowmobile in time to return to the base for his shift.

That night, I lie awake in bed for a long time, despite the exhaustion that sears the space behind my eyes. A lot of people have trouble sleeping at this time of year, thanks to nearly twenty-four-hour daylight, but I know this isn't the reason.

The next day, Keller's waiting for me at the MEC again, and he asks if he can help me count the birds.

"Did you bring me lunch?"

He nods.

"All right, then."

At the colony, I spend more time observing Keller than counting the birds. I watch how carefully he moves among the penguins, clicking their numbers on my counter. I watch his eyes inspect every inch of the carcasses we kneel beside, as I explain how to identify the cause of death. "Only an autopsy can determine if their stomachs are empty," I tell him, pointing at a thin, hollowed-out body, "but you can see here that this one was in really poor condition. Hardly any body fat at all."

I become so absorbed in the work that I fail to notice the wind whipping up around us. It isn't until I feel icy snow pelting my face that I look up and see that there's no longer a delineation between ice and sky, that the world has gone white.

"Shit," I say under my breath, and I radio the station. They've already restricted travel, and the winds are over fifty knots. We need to get back now.

I call out to Keller, and immediately he's at my side, helping me load the snowmobile. Within a few minutes we're ready to go—but the engine won't start.

I try again, the engine grinding slowly but refusing to turn over.

"Dead battery?" Keller asks. He's sitting right behind me, his mouth next to my ear, but I can hardly hear him over the wind.

"Could be," I shout back. "But if it was, I probably wouldn't get any juice at all."

We dismount, and it's then I realize that we don't have time to troubleshoot, let alone to fix the vehicle. The wind is bracing, my hands so cold I can barely move them, even inside my gloves. When I glance back at Keller, only a few feet away, he's a blur, his hat and parka coated with snow.

"We need to take shelter," I say.

"Let me check the battery."

"Forget it, Keller." The driving snow is pricking my eyes. "Even if we fix it now, we're not going to make it back."

While Antarctic weather is notoriously capricious, I'm annoyed; I can't believe I let the storm creep up on us this way. Keller is still going on about fixing the Ski-Doo as I pull our survival pack out of its hutch, and I turn and shove it into his chest. "You have no idea what this weather can do," I shout over the wind. "Get the tent out. Now."

There's no time to dig ourselves a trench, which would be the best way to wait out the storm. As it is, we're barely able to pitch the emergency tent and scurry inside. We've got just one extreme-weather sleeping bag and a fleece liner, and I spread them both out over us. Even if the tent weren't so cramped, the freezing air instinctively draws our bodies close, and without speaking we wrap ourselves up, pulling the fleece to cover us completely, including most of our faces. Despite the protection from the wind and our body heat, it's probably no more than thirty degrees inside the tent.

"I bet this isn't what you had in mind when you came to Antarctica," I say, my voice muffled by the fleece.

"On the contrary," he says. "This is exactly what I had in mind."

I turn slightly toward him in the dim light.

"For God's sake," I say. "You're not worried at all, are you?"

He moves his head slightly, and when he speaks I hear a smile in his voice. "I'm impervious to ice."

This feeling he has—insane, illogical though it is—is one I understand. I'd felt similarly invincible once—at times, my life down here on the continent seemed surreal, a dream-world in which whatever happened remained separate, protected from real life. It's a notion that many who come here can relate to, but it lasts only for a brief time.

"You've read about the continent's history, I take it?" I say. "You know how many bad things have happened here."

"Plenty of miracles, too."

"Is that what you're hoping for?"

"Not really," he says. He pauses, then adds, "Maybe."

"What do you mean?"

"I know I'm not the first one who's come here for a change of scenery. Midlife crisis sort of stuff."

"Definitely not."

"You wouldn't have recognized me three years ago," he says. "I was a lawyer. Married. Nice house outside of Boston. Everything most people want."

"Everything my mother wanted for me, that's for sure," I say. "So what happened?"

A pause, and then he says, "The unthinkable happened."

He goes quiet. I listen to the rhythm of our breathing,

barely audible over the keening of the wind outside. I can tell he is still awake, and I ask, "You okay?"

"Yeah," he says. "You?"

I nod, and we're close enough that my head nudges against his. We fall silent again, snuggled together like puppies for warmth. As time drifts, I think back on the day's work, and then I sit up with a start.

"What is it?"

"My notebook," I say, patting my parka, trying to recall whether I'd stashed it in one of the oversize pockets. "I don't remember where I put it."

"It's in the hutch."

"Are you sure?"

"I saw you put it away."

I stare at the opening of the tent, though I know it would be foolish to venture outside. "I hope it hasn't blown away."

"It won't. You secured it tight."

I wonder then if he's been watching me as closely as I've watched him.

"Relax," he says. I feel his hand on my back, and when I lie down, his arm remains around my shoulders. I feel the day's exertion, finally, take over, draining my body and mind of what little energy is left. I turn toward Keller, and my icy nose meets the warmth of his neck.

I let my breathing slow, but my eyes remain open wide, fixed on the stubble on Keller's face, on the spot where his earlobe joins the skin of his jaw. I never imagined I'd find myself in a situation like this again—in a tent with another civilian, another amateur—and a part of me is afraid to sleep, afraid to risk waking up alone.

I don't remember closing my eyes, but I wake hours later to a bright gold glow. For a long moment, I don't move, savoring the heat of Keller's body next to mine. When I sit up, he stirs and opens his eyes. The look on his face is one I haven't seen in a while—sleepy, not quite sure where he is, a hint of a smile as he remembers.

But it's not me he's smiling about; he's looking past me, at the shadow hovering over my shoulder against the backlit tent.

"The snow," he says. "Look how high those drifts are."

Outside the tent, the sun is a halo behind thin clouds, and a light wind lifts the snow, surrounding us with sparkling dust.

We have to kick the snow away to step out of the tent, and I'm glad I'd remembered, at the last minute, to bury a flagged pole in the snow near the Ski-Doo, which is now hidden under several feet of snow. I radio the station to check in, let them know we'll be on our way soon. By the time I turn back, Keller's uncovered the snowmobile and is bent over the engine.

"I think the spark plugs got iced over when the temps dropped yesterday," he says, straightening up. "Clean and dry now. Give it a try."

The engine starts right up. I let it run while I pack our tent. As we head toward the base, with Keller sitting behind me, his arm around my waist, I wish we weren't on our way back. The cold, exhaustion, and hunger don't compare to my sudden desire to remain with Keller, away from the busyness of the station.

As we return the snowmobile to the MEC and set off for our dorms, I try not to delude myself into thinking he's more interested in me than in the birds. In fact, when I see him later and he suggests we meet at the Southern Exposure, one of McMurdo's bars, he asks if I can bring my notes, if I'd mind sharing them.

And so, over the next couple of weeks, we continue our routine—days counting birds together, nights in the bar after his cafeteria shift. We get to know each other slowly, drink by drink. Once we're a few beers into the night, the conversation becomes personal. Keller doesn't like to talk about himself, and I have to fit together his pre-Antarctic life in puzzle pieces. It's an image that remains with me when I see him each morning—a faded cardboard picture with the seams still visible, the cracks still open.

But I want to put the puzzle together; I want to understand who he is. He's unlike most men I've known, men whose experience here is more academic. Keller seems to go about discovering Antarctica like one of the early-twentieth-century explorers, part fearlessness, part eagerness, and part ambition, as if he's got something to prove. I'm intrigued, as if I've unearthed a new species, one I'm eager to study, bit by bit.

One night I'm gazing at him, trying to picture it—the buttoned-down life he said he'd once lived—this man I've never seen in anything but denim, flannel, and Gore-Tex, whose hands are chapped from nights working in the galley and days counting penguins.

"So you were a lawyer, married, house in the suburbs," I say, wanting the rest of his story. "Kids?"

He says nothing, and something in his face makes me wish I could withdraw the question. I stand up and wobble my way over to the bar to get us another round of drinks. When

I return to the table, he's staring at the wall, at a photo of an emperor colony. Our beers slosh as I put them down on the table, and I tumble into my seat.

Finally he turns to me. "Remember the other day—you told me how penguins that fail to breed will sometimes choose new partners."

For a long moment, I can't comprehend what he's telling me.

"It was our first child," he says. "Only child."

He takes a long drink, and I try to remember how many rounds we've had. "She died," he says. "Car accident."

I don't know what to say. He is very drunk, and he's talking far more than he ever has, yet his body remains still, lean and almost statuesque in the chair. "I thought we might try to have another baby," he says. "But she decided to try another husband."

"Just like that?" As I look at Keller through the bar's haze of cigarette smoke, I'm finding it impossible to imagine anyone walking away from him so easily.

"Just like the birds," he says with a harsh laugh. "I can't blame her."

I want to touch him then, but I don't move.

He shifts in his seat and pushes his hair off his forehead in a slow, tired motion. "It was my fault," he says. "Ally was nineteen months old. Britt, my wife—she went back to work after Ally's first birthday, and we took turns dropping her off at day care, picking her up. I was supposed to pick her up that afternoon, but a meeting got rescheduled. I called our babysitter, Emily—a grad student who took care of Ally from time to time. Ally loved her. I even bought an extra car seat so Emily could take her places. She used to joke we were killing her love life, with a baby seat in her car. It was this crappy old subcompact. If only I'd bought her a new car instead."

He reaches for his beer, but he doesn't pick it up, doesn't drink. "I had my phone off during the meeting. I went home and no one was there—no Ally, no babysitter, no Britt. Then I turned on my phone."

His hand tightens around the glass. "I went to Children's," he says, "but she was gone. A driver on a cell phone had run a red light and slammed into the back, on Ally's side. Emily survived. Britt blamed me more than anyone. I was the one who should've been there."

I reach over and touch his hand, still wrapped around the glass, his skin rough and wind-chapped, and I think of how Antarctica toughens you up, how maybe this was what he wanted—maybe this is what we all want—to build calluses over old wounds.

He turns slightly in his chair, leaning almost imperceptibly closer to me. "It didn't fall apart all at once," he says. "It's strange, how people disappear. No one likes to talk about it— as if it might be catching. Our friends, Britt's and mine, didn't know what to do—I mean, all of a sudden, we didn't have kids who played together anymore. My sister was the only one who would listen, really listen. She's the only one who calls me on Ally's birthday. The only one who invited us over for dinner on the first anniversary of her death, so we wouldn't have to be alone. She's good that way, like my mom was. Everyone else—they seemed to want to pretend it never happened."

He lifts his shoulders in a shrug. "Britt and I tried to make the marriage work. She couldn't move on—or didn't want to. We didn't last much more than a year. After she left, I tried to immerse myself in work." He looks down into his beer. "When we were together, when Ally was alive, the days always seemed too short—there was never enough time to fit it all in. Then, all of a sudden, every day was endless. Nothing seemed to matter anymore. I wanted to escape—like Britt had, I guess. But she only went as far as Vermont."

He takes in a breath. "I started reading about the explorers, you know, wondering whether there was any uncharted territory left. Even by the time I decided to leave the country, I didn't really know where I would go. I didn't have a plan." He pauses, and a small, sad smile emerges on his face. "Looking back, I guess I did know. I remember the day I went into my boss's office and handed over my resignation," he says. "I told him, 'I am just going outside and may be some time.'"

I know, of course, that these were the last words of Captain Lawrence Oates, who died along with Robert Scott and the rest of the expedition team on their return from the South Pole. Knowing he was near death anyhow and a liability to his party, Oates walked out of his tent and onto the ice. No one ever saw him again.

Eventually I tell Keller about Dennis, and he's not surprised; he'd known all along. "I remember reading about it," he says, "and seeing your picture. I thought about how alike we were, even though I'd never met you before."

"Alike how?"

"Abandoned," he says.

Antarctica gets her icy claws into a certain type of person, I've realized over the years, and I can see now that Keller is one of them. Now that he's caught, he'll return again and again, and he'll learn that no one back home can quite understand what brings him here—the impulse to return to the ice; to these waddling, tuxedo-feathered creatures; to the hours-long fiery sunsets; to the soothing wild peace of this place—and he'll eventually build his life around Antarctica because he'll feel unfit to live anywhere else.

That night, we leave the bar as usual, and my heartbeat stutters as we're about to part because I notice the way his eyes are latched to mine. But though his gaze lingers for a moment, he offers only his usual good-bye: a quick wave and a quicker smile.

The next afternoon, we hike up to a ridge overlooking the Ross Ice Shelf—a massive, flat blanket of ice stretching out into the ocean. Though it's the size of France and hundreds of feet thick, it looks as thin as a wafer from high up, and about as fragile. From here we have a good view of a large Adélie colony. I watch a smile spread across Keller's face as he studies them through the binoculars. "I love their faces," he says. "Those eyes."

Adélies have completely black heads, and the tiny white feathers surrounding their glossy black eyes give them a wide-eyed, startled look. Compared to the emperors, the Adélies are tiny; making little huffing noises, they walk with their wings sticking out, feet wide, heads high, looking almost comical, whereas the emperors always look so serious, their wings down at their sides, their heads lowered.

"They might be my favorite species," I admit, "if I had to choose."

He lowers his binoculars, then reaches out to touch my sunburned cheek, and that's when he kisses me. It happens quickly—his hand at the back of my neck, the spontaneous meeting of lips—and then time slows and nearly stops, and suddenly my body feels as wet and limpid as melting ice.

Sex at McMurdo happens in stolen moments; it's furtive and quiet, thanks to too-close living quarters, roommates, thin walls. I don't know how many days blur together between that first kiss and the first night we spend in my dorm, but finally, after an aeon of helpless and constantly rising desire, we sneak out of an all-staff party and crowd into the narrow bunk in my room, ravishing each other like sex-starved teenagers, which is also typical of McMurdo residents.

Afterwards, as the bass traveling on the wind from a distant building echoes the thumping of our hearts, in the arid heat of the room, sweat evaporating from our skin, it seems we could be anywhere—but at the same time, I realize this is the only place where our sudden relationship could feel as familiar to me as the icy, moonlike terrain surrounding us outside the room's tiny windows.

In the weeks that follow, we steal time whenever we can— when my roommate is in the field, when Keller's is at work; it becomes difficult, at other times, to think of anything else. When we come in from the field, we have to peel off so many layers I think we'll never find skin, until there it is, burning under our hands, dry and hot, two deserts finding water.

Under the days' perpetual sunlight, we compile data, we eat and talk, we pack up and hurry back for his shift in the galley. Late one afternoon, when he has the day off, we stretch out in the blinding light, hands folded together, my head on his shoulder, and we listen to the whistling of the wind across the ice and the cries of the birds. I savor the utter silence under those sounds; there is nothing else to hear—none of the usual white noise of life on other continents, no human sounds at all—and Keller and I, too, are silent. It feels as if our own humanness has dissolved, as if we have no need to communicate other than by breath and touch. And I feel the chill that has always seemed a constant and necessary part of me finally begin to thaw.

AS I DRESS in the dark, what seemed like a good idea earlier now seems silly, impractical. I fumble to find my sunglasses and hear my roommate turn over in her bunk, and I'm thinking about taking off my cold-weather gear and getting back into bed myself.

I tiptoe to the door and, in the ray of light from the hall, I glance back at my roommate—still asleep, thick orange earplugs filling her ears, a slumber mask over her eyes—and slip out of the room.

At Keller's dorm, I knock quietly, hoping his roommate doesn't answer. I wait, then knock again, wondering if I've overestimated us, to be so certain he'll welcome a middle-of-the-night surprise wake-up call, that he'll be willing to sacrifice one of the more precious resources of McMurdo summers: sleep.

Finally the door cracks open, and he stands there blinking as the hall's fluorescent lights hit his eyes.

"Get your coat," I whisper.

He shuts the door and a few moments later opens it again, fully dressed. We slink through the dorm. Outside, we shade our eyes from the nighttime sun, still high in the sky and obscured by a veil of wispy clouds. It's about twenty degrees out, maybe colder.

I love that Keller hasn't asked a single question about where we're going, why he's out in the broad daylight of three in the morning. He's just letting me lead the way.

We walk toward Hut Point, a little more than three hundred yards away. The land under our boots is black and white, volcanic earth and frost. The ice-snagged waters of McMurdo Sound stretch out in front of us—and before that: a plain, weathered square building.

The hut that Keller has been so eager to see was built in 1902 for Scott's *Discovery* expedition. For months it's been closed and locked to all but the conservation team that's finishing its restoration—except for tonight.

I dig into my jacket and pull out a key. I let it dangle between us.

His still-sleepy face breaks into a smile. "How'd you get that?"

"I'm well connected."

He grins, and I hand him the key.

Under the awning Keller pulls off his hat, pushing his sunglasses up over his head. He unlocks the door, and we step inside, standing still as we wait for our eyes to adjust to the dim light coming in through the building's small, high windows.

I watch as Keller walks carefully through the hut. I follow his eyes around the soot-blackened room: boxes and tins of oatmeal and cocoa, biscuits and herring; rusted frying pans on the brick stove; shelves scattered with cups and plates, bottles and bowls; oil-smudged trousers hanging on a line, a dog harness from a beam. A pile of dark, oozing seal blubber drips with oil; seal carcasses hang, well preserved, on one of the walls. A large box labeled LAMP OIL reads, SCOTT'S ANTARCTIC EXPEDITION 1910 — one of several other parties that once inhabited this place.

It's eerily noiseless — the hum of the station gone, no penguins outside, no petrels above. Instead of the diesel fumes of the station, we breathe in the thick, musty flavors of hundred-year-old burnt blubber and the dusty artifacts of men whose time here was both celebratory and desperate.

Keller knows not to touch anything, and he moves as little as possible, taking in everything he can. I hadn't thought to bring a camera with me — but then I realize, in all our time together, I've never once seen him take a photograph.

"Remember the lost men?" Keller asks.

"You'll have to be more specific."

"The Ross Sea Party," he says. "They were right here — in this room — never knowing they'd devoted their lives to a lost cause."

"They knew the risks." In 1915, ten men from the Ross Sea Party, the group Shackleton had tasked with laying supply depots for his *Endurance* expedition, had gotten stranded when their ship lost its moorings and drifted. Not knowing that Shackleton's crew had been forced to abandon their own ship, the men kept going, completing their mission, but three of them didn't survive.

"That's exactly what I appreciate about being down here," Keller says. "You know the risks — the hazards are tangible." He takes another look around, as if what he's trying to say is written on the time-scarred walls. "Back in Boston, I was living this so-called normal life, blissfully ignorant of the dangers all around us. That's so much worse. Because when something does happen, you're not prepared for it."

I move closer, and he pulls me into a long hug, so long I feel as if maybe he's afraid to let go — as if by clinging to me, in this hut, in this faraway place, he can preserve his memories and leave them behind at the same time. I want to assure him that he'll find a balance, that it's the same fine line as going from here to home and back again, but I know he'll learn this soon enough, in his own time.

At last he pulls away, kisses my forehead. "Thank you for this," he says.

We go back out into the summer night and walk around the other side of the hut, facing the sound. Clean, cold air freezes through my nostrils, carrying the faint scent of ocean and iced rock.

In the water, flat fragments of ice float around like puzzle pieces; in the distance beyond, thin layers of silver glisten over the light blue of large bergs. As a breeze begins to stir, I lean into Keller, a chill biting through my clothes.

He pulls me closer, staring over the top of my head. "Sea leopard," he whispers, using the explorers' term for the leopard seal that is passing within fifty feet of us, on its way to open water. We watch the seal, a full-grown male, as he propels his sleek gray body forward, focused on the sea ahead.

Then the seal stops and turns his head toward us, sniffing the air, revealing his lighter-gray, speckled underside. He gazes at us, his face like that of a hungry puppy with its wide, whiskered nostrils and huge wet eyes. We're downwind, but

I feel Keller's breath stop halfway through his chest. After a few long moments, the seal turns his head and continues on his way, slipping silently into the water.

Keller exhales, slowly, and I feel his weight settle against me as he relaxes. Though a leopard seal had once hunted a member of Shackleton's *Endurance* party — first on land, then from under the ice — and while they can be highly dangerous, attacks on humans are rare.

I look at Keller, thinking he'd been worried about the seal — and I see he's smiling.

"I could get used to this," he says.

"To what, exactly? Close encounters with deadly predators? The subzero temperatures? The six-day workweeks?"

"You," he says. "I could get used to you."

WITH CONSTANT DAYLIGHT, time loses its urgency, and it's easy for me to believe we'll be here forever. Yet eventually the sun sets for an hour a day, and then a few more — and soon conversations on the base begin to eddy around the transition from summer to winter season. As our time at McMurdo grows shorter, I can't stop myself from thinking ahead. Real life begins to intrude into every moment. Lying in Keller's bed one afternoon, I tuck my head under his chin. "Where do you live now? Back home, I mean?"

We still don't know some of the very basic facts about each other. Here, none of it matters.

"After the divorce, I got an apartment in Boston," he says. "When I came here, I put everything in storage." With my face against his neck, I feel the vibration of his voice almost more than I hear it.

"I have a cottage in Eugene." I curl an arm around his chest, wrap a leg around his. "Plenty of room for two, if you wanted to visit. Or stay."

The moment the words are in the air, I feel myself shrink away from them, anticipating his reaction. I pull the sheet over my bare shoulder, as if this could shield me from hearing anything but yes.

Yet he lifts my chin to look at me, intrigued. "Really?"

"Sure."

A pensive look crosses his face, and I think of his life before, how rich and full it must've been—and now this: a dorm room with frayed sheets and scratchy, industrial woolen blankets, and ahead only the promise of a storage unit in Boston, or a tiny cottage and a wet Oregon spring.

Then he smiles. "Remind me," he says, "how long have you lived alone?"

"We're practically living together here. I've spent more time with you than with any non-penguin in years."

He pulls me up and over until I'm on top of him, looking down at his face. Our weeks here, with long workdays and rationed water, have left him windburned and suntanned, long-haired and scruffy. I lean in close, and he says, "What are we waiting for?"

WE DON'T TALK much about it after that day. I don't think about what Keller might do for work in Oregon, about the fact that he'd only recently begun a whole new life. All I can think about is him coming back with me—the first time I've been able to bring home something I needed, a part of the place that always seems to make me whole.

The last days in Antarctica before heading Stateside usually make me jittery, but this time it's Keller who's on edge during our final week at the station.

"It's always hard to leave," I assure him. "But we'll be back."

"I know *you* will," he says. "You've got a career. I'm just a dishwasher. And everyone wants to be a dishwasher in Antarctica."

He's right; the competition for the most menial jobs at McMurdo is astounding. "But you got here," I say. "You've proven yourself. They'll want you back."

Our last days are busy—I'm gathering my final bits of data and wrapping up the project; Keller, as well as working in the galley, has been filling in for Harry Donovan, one of the maintenance guys, who's been sick. We're spending less and less time together, which doesn't concern me because soon we'll have nothing but time. We're among the last of the summer staff still here—already the base is shrinking down, getting closer to its winter size of two hundred. In six more weeks, the sun will set and not rise again for four months.

When I see Keller at Bag Drag, at the Movement Control Center from where we'll load our bags onto the Terra Bus headed for the airfield, the place is overstuffed with people, cold-weather gear, and luggage—amid all this, Keller looks strangely empty-handed. It's not unusual for flights to be delayed or canceled, but I have a sinking feeling that's not the case. I lower my bags and look around. "Where's your stuff?"

He hasn't spoken, hasn't moved; he's just watching me. "Deb," he says.

His tone, low and cautious, causes my chest to tighten, and I don't want him to say anything more. With my foot, I slide my duffel toward him. "Help me with my bag."

But he doesn't move. "I don't know how to tell you this," he says, "so I'm just going to say it. I'm staying. For the winter."

I sling my laptop bag over my shoulder, keeping my eyes on the floor. I'm afraid to look up at him, as if seeing his face will make what he's telling me real. For the moment, it's all just words in the air.

"Harry's got bronchitis," he goes on, "and he's going home. I'm here, I'm vetted—so they offered me his job." A pause. "It's a step up from dishwashing, at least."

I'm silent, still staring downward.

"I'm not sure if I'll ever make it back here otherwise, you know?" I hear a pleading note in his voice. "Come on, Deb, say something."

I look up at him finally. "What's there to say?"

"Tell me you understand."

"I don't."

"I need this, Deb. I've tried to start over—with Britt, with my job—nothing worked. But here"—he raises his hands as if to take in not just the building but the whole continent—"I feel as though it's possible here."

He steps forward, gathers my hands. "You'll be back before you know it. Next season. Or even sooner—for Winfly, maybe," he says, referring to the six-week fly-in period between winter and the main season. "Or I'll see you in Oregon. Like we planned."

When I don't answer, he squeezes my hands. "I'm doing this for my future here. For ours."

When I look at him, I know that he's fallen head over heels—not for me but for this continent. I can't blame him. I myself had overwintered after my first visit to McMurdo. Much like Keller, after I'd gotten a taste of Antarctica, I didn't want to leave. Because there'd been no research for me over the winter—the wildlife disappears when the sea ice encompasses the island—I'd taken a job as a firehouse dispatcher. I'd have done anything to stay.

And I want to tell him so many things. That it's exhilarating—the way the sun dips below the horizon for longer and longer each day, a glowing orange yolk that leaves behind a reddish black sky. That it's lonely—that he will hear the waning sound of the season's last plane echoing in the sky for a long, long time. That it's dangerous—that the storms here are unlike anything he's ever seen, with winds at a hundred knots, temperatures at eighty degrees below zero, snow blasting through the air like violent ghosts and seeping into buildings through the smallest cracks imaginable. That in the six months of total isolation, with no supply deliveries, no company other than two hundred other wintering souls, he will long for things like city streets, oranges, the leaves of trees.

Yet he's made up his mind. While overwintering isn't for the faint of heart, I know Keller believes it will be easier for him to be here than at home. And he's probably right.

I drop his hands and pick up my duffel. I can't speak, so I nudge past him toward the door.

"That's it?" He's speaking to my back as I approach the exit, the sunlight from the open door blindingly bright.

I stop and turn around. "Come with me, Keller. If you stay here . . ."

He comes close, puts a cool hand on my cheek. "It'll be fine," he says. "It's just a few months."

"Six months," I remind him.

"That's nothing, in Antarctic time," he insists.

It's forever, but I don't tell him that. I'm still holding my duffel, which is heavy, and I feel the painful stretching of muscles in my arm as I stand there, waiting for Keller to change his mind, knowing he won't. When he reaches for my bag, I let him take it. We don't talk as I get weighed with my bags, have my passport checked. We share a brief wisp of a kiss, nothing more. Keller waits on the ice as I board the bus, as it rumbles toward the airfield on its massive tires.

As I watch Keller through the bus's small windows, I think of the look on his face when he'd watched the Adélies that day on the ice, the first time he kissed me. I remember telling him that the Adélies will sometimes mate for life, but they are loyal first and foremost to their nesting sites—and now it seems that Keller and I are no different, loyal first and always to the continent.

At McMurdo in the depth of winter, people come together for many reasons—loneliness and boredom even more than attraction and compatibility—and I wonder if Keller will emerge from the dark with another woman in his life, just as at the end of each winter, an Adélie will return to its nest, but if its partner doesn't show, it will choose a new one and move on.

FIVE DAYS BEFORE SHIPWRECK

Aitcho Islands, South Shetland Islands
(62°24'S, 59°47'W)

It's early in the morning when I go up to the ship's "business center," a tiny space with a short row of computer terminals and a satellite phone. On the *Cormorant*, the emphasis is on seeing the sights, not on staying connected, but there's just enough here for the die-hard workaholics to plug in if they need to. From what I've heard about the *Australis*, all the passengers' and crew's quarters have in-room phones, so it should be easy enough to reach Keller.

After an operator connects me, I listen to the ringing of the phone—a strange sound to hear as I look out at nothing but sea and ice. I've never had to reach anyone from the Southern Hemisphere before—everyone back home knows when I'm away and when to expect me back—and this need to connect fills me with an unfamiliar anxiety, as though I've learned a new language and am fumbling to find the right words. As the ringing continues, I wonder: Do these in-room phones have voice mail? And if so, what will I say?

After another moment of static, I hear his voice—clear and familiar.

"Keller, it's me."

"Deb?" He sounds concerned. "What's the matter? Are you all right?"

"You're asking *me* what's the matter?" The worry, the skip in my heart upon hearing his voice, unexpectedly translates to anger, and I can't mask my irritation.

He sighs but says nothing.

"Why didn't you tell me?"

"I thought Glenn might change his—"

"I know, I talked to Glenn," I interrupted.

"I was hoping to see you in Ushuaia, but we set off earlier, and since then it's been so busy I haven't had a moment to think. I've been trying to figure out how to contact you."

"Why the *Australis*? That ship is a bull in a china shop. You know that."

"I needed a job; they needed extra crew. And it gets me closer to you."

I picture his face, in an expression of the innocent, misguided hope that we might actually see each other, and this softens me a bit. "But what are you planning to do, jump ship and steal a Zodiac? I want to see you, too, but how in the world is that going to happen?"

"I'm still working on that part. We're in the same hemisphere, at least."

"I just wish you'd told me," I say. "Back in Eugene. Maybe we both should've stayed home."

"That's exactly why I didn't tell you. You need to be here, just like I do. I'll patch things up with Glenn eventually. I actually think he would've taken me back, if he hadn't been able to find anyone."

"Thom. He found Thom."

"I know."

"Why didn't you just keep your mouth shut?" I'm thinking back to last season, the moment that got him on Glenn's blacklist—our shipboard lecture, the defiant passenger, Keller's short temper—and I wish I could go back and seize the mic from Keller's hands.

"Like you wouldn't have said the same things?" he says.

"But I *didn't*. That's the difference."

"Well, I can't do anything about it now. I'm here. That's what matters."

"Why does it matter so much if we can't be together?"

"You'll see."

"What does that mean?"

"It means you'll know when I see you."

Thoughts sweep through my mind—whether we might actually see each other, whether Keller does have a future with this program—and a moment later he says, "Look, we'll figure it out. Let's talk later, all right?"

I'm not ready to let him go; I want to ask, *When? How?* But before I can get the words out, the line goes dead. I'm not sure whether we've been disconnected or Keller has simply hung up.

AS I HEAD toward the dining room to pick up a quick bite before our scheduled landing, I'm still arguing with Keller in my head, changing words and sentences, hoping for a different outcome. Our voices rising. The line going silent.

Then I stop—the voices are real, and they're apparently coming from a couple just inside one of the hatches to the outer decks. I don't want to listen, but I can't pass without interrupting, so I wait, hoping they'll move on, or at least reconcile quickly.

After a moment, I recognize the voices—Kate and Richard Archer.

"If you don't want to do the landing, why on earth did we come down here?" she's saying. "Why come all this way if you don't even care?"

"For you," he says. "You wanted this trip."

"I wanted something for us. To get reacquainted, Richard. Not just to be on a boat with a hundred other people. To go for a walk, to see the penguins, to see their chicks, to—I don't know, share a moment together."

"Do you remember how we met?" he asks.

"What are you talking about?" She sounds exasperated. "Of course I do."

"That day in the café, when your computer crashed. You had a memory leak."

"Richard, can we talk about this later?"

"Let me finish," he says, his voice louder.

"Okay, okay." She speaks in a whisper, as if she might be able to quiet him by example.

"The software was eating up your laptop's memory," he continues. "That's why it crashed. It was an easy fix, but you didn't know that. I wanted you to think I was a hero."

"What are you saying? You don't think I value you enough?"

"No, I'm saying that this trip, this sudden obsession with the penguins and the melting ice, it's like a memory leak," he says. "It's consuming your mind, our plans—"

"Richard—"

"To retire early. To start a family."

"No," she says. "*You* wanted to retire, not me. And you've earned it. About the baby—I never said never. I just wanted to talk about it some more, that's all."

There's a pause, and then Richard says, "I thought we'd already made the decision."

"We aren't like your computers, Richard. Our life is not a software program. We're allowed to change our minds, to change our plans."

"Except that you're the only one changing," he says. "I've held up my end of the bargain. What about you?"

"What *about* me? You're bargaining with yourself, Richard. You've left me completely out of it. And that's not my fault."

He doesn't answer, and I hear the slamming of the hatch, which means that at least one of them has gone out to the deck. I wait a little longer, until I'm certain they both must be gone, and then I continue on to the dining room. Breakfast is in full swing, but I don't see either one of them.

LANDINGS ARE METICULOUSLY organized in order to appear efficient and seamless. Glenn and Captain Wylander find a spot to anchor, a place to land the Zodiacs. Glenn gives us a timetable, since he has to coordinate everything with the galley as well; due to the ever-changing weather, the chance to go ashore takes precedence over scheduled mealtimes. A few naturalists set off to scout trails for hiking, to make sure there are no leopard seals napping nearby. We find the best place to bring passengers ashore—preferably a shallow beach where we can haul the Zodiacs as close to dry land as possible.

The passengers, meanwhile, line up in the B Deck passageway leading to the mudroom, where they'll sterilize their boots and move magnetic tags with their names and cabin numbers from an ON SHIP to an OFF SHIP position. It's low tech, unlike the *Australis*-style ships that have electronic swipe cards for everything, but it helps us make sure every passenger who leaves the ship eventually gets back on.

The Aitcho Islands are an ideal place to land—plenty of penguins, fairly even terrain. As I lead a group of tourists away from the landing site, the chinstraps roam all around, their webbed feet leaving watery prints in the thick mud near the shore. I issue a strict warning not to go near the birds—but I can see how tempting it might be to pet them, to feel their silky black heads and snowy white faces, to trace the thin black lines encircling the undersides of their chins. The adult penguins, with no predators on land, will often pass close by; sometimes they'll even walk right up to you. We constantly need to remind passengers that this is not a marine park, that we're actually in the wild. Sometimes Keller will show them his ragged penguin-bite scars, which works pretty well as a deterrent.

When it comes to the tourists, our patience can wear thin, Keller's especially—but I'm always reminding him that while we've grown used to this environment, for everyone else it's like a cold, faraway planet that probably doesn't feel quite real.

And, more important, what people learn here might actually make a difference if they go home thinking about how much their actions up north affect the creatures down here.

I point to the guano that covers the nests and rocks, and now covers our boots as well—its sharp, overwhelming stench is the reason many of the passengers have covered their noses with scarves or the tops of their sweaters. "You'll see how the guano is a reddish pink over there, where the chinstraps are," I say. "That means they're eating krill. Over here, the color's more whitish pink, which shows the gentoos are eating fish as well as krill. What we don't like to see is guano that's a greenish color, which indicates a bird is starving."

We continue our hike. The hills are studded with nests of rocks and pebbles, and penguins with fat, gray-and-white chicks are nestled up against them. Kate is in my group—Richard is not—and I can't help thinking of what I'd overheard earlier. I feel sorry for her, for both of them, and, for once, I can relate to such relationship issues: to one person wanting something the other doesn't, to missed connections. I'd finally begun to feel that Keller and I were past all that, yet here we are, with him in one place and me in another, not knowing whether we'll be able to find our way back.

I feel a sudden lurch of nausea and pause midstep. Perplexed, I take a breath and try to steady myself. Despite the jet lag, despite the Drake, despite all the passengers and crew crowded together on these trips, I never get sick. And I don't like the thought that I'm getting myself this worked up over Keller.

One of the tourists asks if I'm all right, and I shake it off and keep walking.

At the crest of the hill, we stop and look out over the bay. Beyond lies a sea of rich blue, the water broken by ice and lava flats, the skyline broken by the sharp, ice-blanched peaks of the rugged island chain. I direct the tourists' attention below, to where gentoos and elephant seals share a beach of thick, volcanic sand and fist-size rocks.

I watch Kate, who stares ahead as if she hasn't heard me, as if she's not aware of the giant, belching, molting seals, their smooth, shiny coats emerging underneath a thick, peeling brown layer that's more pungent than the penguin guano. The seals, under the sun's steady glow, use their flippers to fling sand over their bodies, grunting with every move. The humans are wearing hats, gloves, boots, and several layers under thick parkas, but for the animals, it's too warm. The white-bellied gentoo chicks, still fluffy without their insulating adult feathers, are panting in the heat.

The birds are especially active today, and we proceed back to the beach, more slowly than I'd usually walk because my stomach is still threatening to rebel. Once the shoreline is in sight, I let the group go ahead to the landing site and hang back to radio Glenn.

"I need to come back," I tell him. "I'm not feeling well."

"What's the matter?"

It's the first time I have ever called in sick. "I'm sure it's nothing," I say, but I can't explain further than that.

"I'll send someone out to take your place," Glenn says. "I want you to see Susan when you get back to the ship."

I know I don't need a doctor, but I also know better than to argue with Glenn.

As I make my way to the Zodiacs, I watch the chinstraps

continue their shuffle from their colony down to the shoreline, where they wade in, then dive under and vanish in swirls of water. Other birds emerge, shaking the water off their backs, and head back up to the colony. The cycle continues, over and over, and all of a sudden something feels familiar in their consistent path, in their methodical gait. I see my own life in theirs: a constant back-and-forth motion, always ending up where I started, and circling back again—focused and simple—and perhaps this is why I chose this life, for the straightforward beauty I'm witnessing right now. Maybe I thought that life down here would remain uncomplicated, and that I could keep the same pace, the same arm's-length existence from the world, forever.

TWO YEARS BEFORE SHIPWRECK

Ushuaia, Argentina

I arrive in Ushuaia late, and by the time I reach the docks I'm a full day behind everyone else and horribly jet-lagged. I'm still on the gangway, holding my duffel bag, as Glenn begins to introduce me to a new crew member. I don't recognize the tall, dark-haired man Glenn calls over until he turns around.

The red bandanna around his neck. The mossy brown eyes.

"Keller Sullivan," Glenn says, "Deb Gardner."

"We've already met," Keller says, extending a hand.

I take it. Keller's hand, ungloved, is warm and rough. I let my eyes hover on his.

"Briefly," I say, withdrawing my hand. "A while back."

I haven't seen Keller since the day I left him at McMurdo, two years ago. He looks at once the same and different—still beautiful, his skin a little more weathered, his stubble a little scruffier. Most noticeable of all, he exudes a confidence he hadn't had before. He looks as though he belongs here.

Keller had e-mailed me faithfully from the station during

his austral winter, and over my own long, humid summer in Eugene, I tried to understand his decision, to put myself in his shoes. I even envisioned him on that bus instead of me, pictured myself staying behind for months of lightless cold while he left for home alone. Yet I wasn't sure I'd have been able to make that decision as effortlessly as he had.

We had only talked once; phone calls were expensive and hard to coordinate; with limited bandwidth, Skype wasn't allowed. After that first call, after I could no longer see Keller's face or hear his voice, as he wrote about overwintering—the biting chill, the inky dark, the supernatural green light of the aurora australis—he only seemed farther and farther away.

His choosing to stay made sense to me—he'd suffered losses that would never fully heal, and perhaps he thought the austral winter in Antarctica would help because, with the onset of darkness, the notion of time disappears along with the sun. That he could trade our plans so easily for an overwinter at McMurdo proved that he was ready to build a new life for himself, but it was one that didn't include me.

I had worked hard to let him go, and I'm wholly unprepared to see him again, here on the *Cormorant*, though I should've known it would happen. Antarctica is a small world.

After introducing us, Glenn leaves us standing there.

"What are you doing here?" I ask.

"I have a job, same as you."

"You could've told me, at least."

"How?" Keller says. "You stopped writing me back. You didn't return my calls."

I look down at my hands, red from the chill in the air, and try to settle the thoughts swarming through my head, to articulate what I want to say. "It seemed pretty clear that was what you wanted, by staying at the base, then going back to Boston—"

"I only went back to Boston because I hadn't heard from you. Where was I supposed to go?"

"It's fine; I get it," I say. "You did what you had to do. So did I."

A crackle through Keller's radio startles us both, and he pulls it from his waist—it's Glenn, calling with a chore.

"Can we talk later?" Keller asks, and I shrug.

Despite my casual gesture, the knowledge that Keller is on board stays with me every second. The day is chaotic, with my attention pulled in myriad directions—helping the expedition team sketch out a rough itinerary, gathering data and photos for the presentations I'll give during the journey, pitching in wherever I'm needed—and I see Keller only in passing, within groups of crew members or other naturalists. Yet my heart rate quickens at the sight of him—and even when he's not around, I feel his proximity like an electric current, a frayed wire, loose and dangerous.

Finally, after the ship is prepped and everything quiets down, I go out to the uppermost deck, the one reserved for crew. In the evening dusk, I look at Tierra del Fuego as thick clouds hover over the mountains and creep down amid the sunset-hued buildings of Ushuaia. Opposite are the calm waters of the Beagle Channel, from where we'll begin our journey tomorrow evening.

I hear the creak of a hatch opening, then the sound of footsteps on the deck. It's Keller approaching, smiling just as I remember—a quick, easy smile with a hint of sadness underneath. He carries a worn paperback in his gloved hands. Seeing him, I feel a familiar cool hollowness, like an ice fog settling into a valley—the way I'd felt long after leaving him at McMurdo.

I'd kept busy the spring after I left, working on my data and writing a paper on my findings at the Garrard colony; when the days in Oregon grew long and bright, I taught a summer school class and then got a last-minute gig in the Galápagos on another ship from the *Cormorant*'s tour company. I'd returned to Antarctica as usual last season, and being on the peninsula felt far enough from Ross Island that I managed not to think too much about Keller. By then, I didn't know where he was; I'd let our correspondence go months earlier.

Now, as I look at him on the deck, with the breeze in his hair and his eyes fixed on mine, it seems as if time has frozen, as if I'm back in the same moment at the Movement Control Center at McMurdo, when he told me he was staying behind.

He holds up his book, its pages fluttering in the night's breeze. *Alone* by Richard Byrd. I'd read the book years ago, a memoir by the first person who'd wintered by himself on the continent.

"The first time I read this," Keller says, "it was about two years after Ally died, after Britt and I split up. I came across Byrd's home address—it's right there in the book—and I knew exactly where it was. He lived on Brimmer Street, in Beacon Hill, not even a mile away from me."

He palms the book between his hands. "I was still at my old job, so the next morning, I worked a half day from home, then headed over to Beacon Hill on my way to the office. It wasn't hard to find the address, but I began to doubt it was Byrd's real house because there wasn't a plaque or anything setting it apart—and this was the home of a man who had three ticker-tape parades in his honor during his lifetime, and a state funeral after he died, a man who's buried in Arlington National Cemetery. So I was about to keep walking when a woman emerged from the house with a bag of garbage. I said hello and blurted out that I was admiring her house. Without missing a beat, she said, 'So you've read the book.' I said yes, and then she invited me in for a tour."

Keller's lips turn up in a half smile. "She showed me the paneled library on the first floor with a carved oak fireplace mantel, where Byrd planned his journeys. She showed me the little backyard where Byrd tried to keep penguins after one of his trips. It was unbelievable that she did that—she didn't know me; I could've been any kind of lunatic. But I knew why when I told her she should put a plaque up on the building. She shrugged and said, 'Nobody remembers Byrd anyway.'" Keller looks up, his eyes meeting mine. "That was the day I quit my job. I wanted to do something worth remembering."

"And so you became a dishwasher at McMurdo."

He smiles. "I thought of it as a temporary distraction—the part where I got away from it all and discovered what I wanted to do. I had no idea this would be what I really wanted. Which meant I had to start over, catch up to you."

"You thought leaving me was the best way?"

"For the record, I never planned to stay on," he says. "I never wanted to separate, but that was my chance—to learn as much as I could, to become something new. I tried to explain it. If only you'd picked up the phone."

He steps closer, leaning his body next to mine against the railing. "I wasn't ready to go home. Not then."

"But you weren't planning to go home," I say. The cry of a petrel in the distance adds a background whining note to my voice. "You were planning to come to Oregon with me."

"And wash dishes in Eugene?"

"There were other options. Other ways to come back down here."

"Like what? By staying, I could put the hours in, learn how things worked. Whenever I wasn't working, I was out helping anyone who needed it."

"So why'd you leave McMurdo at all?"

"Because that was only the beginning of the journey." He takes my cold hands, and I don't resist. "You were the destination."

I shake my head, my mind trying to return to the way it was between us, wanting to get it all back.

"What is it?" Keller asks.

"Just trying to remember the last time you kissed me."

Keller puts a hand on one side of my face, and as he slips his hand to the back of my neck, he pulls me forward and kisses me, a long slow deep kiss that in an instant melts away the icy edges that had frozen since I left McMurdo.

Finally he steps back and looks at me. "So," he says, with that grin of his. "Does that jog your memory?"

I try to look nonchalant, though my hands are shaking. "Vaguely."

He kisses me again, and we stay out on the deck for a long time, huddled together, trying to fit the past two years into the next two hours as night settles over Ushuaia.

It doesn't take us long to pick up where we'd left off—and, as at McMurdo, our time together is so unpredictable, so divided among shipboard duties, that every moment feels tenuous, as if we might easily lose each other again.

Over late nights on the crew deck, Keller fills me in on what he's been up to the past two years: He'd done legal consulting as he went back to school full-time, earning a master's in ecology, behavior, and evolution in only two semesters. He wrote his thesis on the impact of rising global temperatures on Adélies, and he impressed the APP enough for them to recommend him to Glenn as a naturalist this season so that he could gather data on Petermann Island.

I'd known that, with Thom taking time off, I'd have a new research partner on Petermann, but I'd assumed it would be one of the long-timers from the APP. And then, after six whirlwind days on board the *Cormorant*, one of the other naturalists escorts Keller and me to the island by Zodiac, with two weeks' worth of supplies.

As soon as the *Cormorant* recedes into the Penola Strait, Keller and I work quickly to establish our small camp, pitching all three tents though we know one will remain empty. After a week of pent-up sexual energy on board, we're both eager to take advantage of being alone, at last. As I lie naked in the tent, my body awakening in the cool air, under Keller's hands, I realize the extent to which I'd let myself grow numb, forgetting the pleasures to be found in my own skin. The tent is tight and cramped, not unlike our individual sleeping quarters on the *Cormorant*—but now, rather than the hum of the ship, we hear the sounds of the penguins and waves lapping the bay; rather than dry heated air, the night is alive with a gelid summer mist. It's effortless, being together again, as if it were days later rather than years, and the emotional scrim that had begun to envelop me falls away again. Keller, too, seems more at peace, as though he has shed the very last of his former self, traces of which I'd seen when we first met. Now he's only muscle and bone, as if distilled down to his very essence—the part of him I still feel may be just out of my reach.

In the morning, we rise early; it's a balmy forty degrees, and we work in light jackets, forgoing hats and gloves. Our tasks for the next two weeks include counting birds, eggs, and chicks, as well as weighing a sampling of chicks to contribute to one of our ongoing studies on the connections among penguin populations and factors like climate change, food sources, the fishing industry, local weather, oil spills.

We've continued to examine the effects of tourism on the birds. Two hundred years ago, the penguins had the continent all to themselves; now they come into contact with bacteria they have no defenses for. Four years ago, Thom and I tested tourists' boots as they boarded after a landing and found almost two dozen contaminants. Glenn wasn't at all happy about our stopping guests from the Zodiacs on their way to lunch, so that was our first and last experiment. And in truth, we can't blame only tourism; migrating birds bring new toxins, too—we've found salmonella and *E. coli*, West Nile and avian pox. Still, whether it's climate change or tourism, the only thing not changing is the penguins' vulnerability. So we keep studying, and I keep wondering what impact our data might have.

Seeing Keller working nearby throughout the long days, sharing our meals, retreating to our tent as dusk settles over the island—all this has given me a sense of optimism I haven't felt since my early years here. For so long I've identified with the continent in its icy despair, the ephemeral nature of its wildness—but I feel newly energized, as if what we accomplish here may make a difference after all.

The weather holds up for nearly our entire stay—it isn't until the last day that an icy rain begins to fall midafternoon, while we're still in the midst of the day's work. The adult penguins are unfazed, going about their business as the raindrops roll off their feathered backs—but the chicks, still covered with dark-gray fluff, can't shake out the water that sinks into their down, and many of them will freeze to death this year.

Keller and I are both as waterlogged as the chicks when he convinces me it's time to give in; the temperature is dropping, the rain turning to sleet. We scurry into our tight two-person tent, where Keller takes off his boots and helps me with mine. We toss our dripping jackets into the corner, on top of the boots, as we shiver in the frigid air.

"Lie back," Keller says. He pushes my shirt up over my shoulders, and I close my eyes, trying to stop my body's shaking as I feel his mouth on my belly, my breasts, my neck, then holding my breath as he travels downward. With his tongue he limns the angles and curves of my body, filling the hollow places he'd left behind, until new tremors flood through me, washing away all but the two of us, our bodies damp and drying in the wind-rattled tent.

Later, when the rain stops, we hang our clothes to dry outside. I'm quiet, thinking about what comes next. After our return voyage, when the *Cormorant* docks in Ushuaia, we'll watch the passengers crowd onto a coach bus bound for the airport, and we'll have one more night together before Keller himself heads to the airport. Because this is Keller's first trip with the *Cormorant*, he'd only been offered one voyage, one assignment at Petermann. He'll travel from Ushuaia to Santiago to Miami to Boston while I prepare for the next group of passengers to embark. I'll spend another week on board and two more weeks on Petermann with another naturalist from the APP before heading back to the States myself.

"Don't worry," he says, as if reading my mind, as we begin a walk along the edge of the gentoo colony near our camp. "It won't be like before. We'll figure things out."

He stops, looking out over the colony, then raises his hands, as if framing the scene for a photograph. "All this — it reminds me of a word I learned from my grandmother, a long time ago," he says. "Her parents were German immigrants, and this was back when there was a lot of anti-German feeling in the States, so they distanced themselves from their heritage. My grandmother had always wanted to visit Germany, but she never did — she taught me this German word, *fernweh*, which doesn't have an equivalent word in English. It means something like being homesick for a place you've never been. She said that was how she felt about Germany, her whole life." He motions toward the hills, peppered with nesting gentoos. "I finally understand what she meant."

A looming intuition seeps from below my consciousness, like the weighty, hidden part of an iceberg — the unwelcome awareness that for Keller, this is still about Antarctica, not about me. The continent has given him the unexpected liberty of beginning again — and while I know I can never understand the depth of his loss, I'm not sure he can truly begin again, even if he doesn't fully realize it. He'd let me go once already, by staying at McMurdo, and, though I'd managed to let him go, too, I won't be able to do it twice.

"So is there a word in English—in any language—for what we're doing?" I ask. "For thinking we can make it work this time?"

"Insanity?" he says.

I laugh. "The ecstatic display," I say, thinking of penguin mating rituals. "The flipper dance."

"Normal people," he says, "just call it love."

WE MEET UP late in the day, at the edge of one of the island's largest gentoo colonies, each of us clutching a hand counter. We settle on a large, flat rock about twenty feet from the colony to rest for a few minutes before heading back to camp.

We watch a crèche of juveniles waddle eagerly forward as adult penguins return from the sea, ready to feed their still-dependent offspring. A few penguins sit on eggs, and others are feeding very young chicks, taking turns to forage for food. One gentoo tries to steal rocks from another's nest, evoking a shrieking match among several of the birds. A skua lands dangerously close to a nest, stepping toward one of the tiny chicks, and five nearby gentoos turn on the skua, who lets out a rubbery caw and flaps away. Moments later, the gentoos are squawking at one another again.

"I'm still getting used to not intervening," Keller says.

One of the challenges of being a naturalist is letting nature take its course, no matter what. "I'm not sure that feeling ever leaves you."

He lifts his eyes from the penguins to the ocean beyond. "One day at McMurdo," he says, "a Weddell seal wandered onto the base—I have no idea how he got there, so far away from the water. He was all alone, just sort of limping along. He was small—a juvenile."

I listen, remembering when we met, when Keller couldn't tell a crabeater seal from a Weddell. How he'd called the leopard seal a sea leopard.

"I followed him, wanting to help. There was no way I could get him back to the water, but I could tell he was dying, and I wished I could put him out of his misery, at least. I stayed back, waiting, as he slinked along. I don't know if he was aware of me or not. Finally he stopped moving. I watched him die." Keller turns his head toward me. "Is that crazy?"

"I'd have done the same." I stretch out my legs until one of my thick-soled boots touches his. Those who winter over at McMurdo occasionally see animals heading away from the sea when they should be going toward it—some are confused, lost; others are steady and determined, as if they are on some strange suicidal mission. Of all the challenges of overwintering, this is the most disconcerting.

"I'm sorry I didn't stay in touch," I say. "I was trying to protect myself, I guess."

"I shouldn't have given you a reason to."

I nudge his boot. "Only one more week until we're back in Ushuaia."

"I wish I could stay down here," he says.

"I can give you the key to my cottage," I suggest. "You can

make yourself at home. The place does need a good cleaning, though, and you'll have to feed my landlord's cat."

He smiles. "Can I take a rain check?"

"Why?"

"I'll be teaching at Boston University, believe it or not—just summer term, a freshman bio course. When they offered it to me a month ago, I didn't know whether I'd see you. After we lost touch, I thought—" He stops. "It's a different sort of complicated, this life, isn't it?"

I think of two volcanologists I know from McMurdo, an "ice couple," meaning they are together whenever they're at the station but then happily return home to their families, thousands of miles apart, after their research time ends—an arrangement not at all uncommon among Antarctic researchers and staff.

"Couldn't you get out of it?" I ask. "I mean, if you really want to come to Oregon instead."

"I don't know. I guess a part of me needs to see this through."

"Teaching? You could do that in Eugene."

"It's not that. It's about"—he pauses—"not disappearing."

"What do you mean?"

"It's been almost five years," he says, "but still I go home and think of how things used to be. Wiping up Ally's dinner from the kitchen floor while Britt gave her a bath, or vice versa. We traded off these things, but usually we both read her a story. Sometimes it was the only time we all were together in a day, but we always had that." A smile lights his face, and I feel as though he's talking more to himself than to me. Then it fades. "Britt donated all of Ally's books to Children's Hospital before I had a chance to go through them. I'd have liked to keep just one. Her favorite was *Make Way for Ducklings.* Since we lived in Boston and we'd taken her to see the bronze ducks in the Public Garden, she thought it was a true story."

He leans back slightly on the rock, propping himself up with his hands. "After she was gone, after Britt left, I'd be at the office until nine, ten, eleven. Until I was tired enough to know I could get to sleep in an empty apartment. Before I could register how quiet the place was, and how neat—no food on the floor, no toys in the bathtub, no picture books." He angles his head toward mine, though his focus is on a pair of gentoos walking past a few feet away. "Just before I went to McMurdo, I called Britt. A week before Ally would've turned four. Britt had met her new husband by then, but they weren't married yet. I told her I was thinking about her because of Ally's birthday—but the truth was, a part of me was worried that she'd forget. She'd been trying so hard to move on, to erase both of us from her life—it was as if we'd both disappeared." He raises his eyes to mine. "And then I did disappear. I came down here."

There's nothing I can say, and I suddenly feel selfish for wanting all that I want for us, for even attempting to weigh my own desire against the depth of his pain.

I move one of my gloved hands over to touch his and lean against him. We watch a penguin raise her head, calling to her chicks, and they emerge from the crèche, wobbling toward her, ready to eat.

The weather has turned, the wind blasting tiny frozen chips of rain into our faces, our hats and jackets. We sit and watch the penguins for a few more minutes before packing up our supplies and heading back to camp.

THE NEXT MORNING, we're packed and ready by the time Glenn radios with the *Cormorant*'s ETA. Keller and I are windblown and grubby; I feel the sweet, worn-out exhilaration that comes from the end of a research trip, as well as the nagging anxiety about what our data will ultimately reveal.

Keller has already taken a load of supplies to the landing site, and as I follow, approaching the bay where a Zodiac will appear for us at any moment, I feel the same irresistible pull toward Keller I always have, taut as ever. I slow as I get nearer, and the few feet left between us feels vast, wide open; in this space I see our entire relationship, or whatever this actually is—both clear and opaque, entirely comfortable, and completely whole.

An hour later, after a hot shower on board, I glimpse my face in the tiny mirror above the sink. I hardly recognize myself, and it's not the sun- and wind-reddened skin or the dark circles under my eyes or the deepening of a few wrinkles. With a jolt I recall learning, in a long-ago biology class, about a section of the cerebral cortex that, when damaged, causes a condition known as face blindness. If you damage this part of the brain, you can no longer recognize friends, family members, or even your own face in the mirror—and this is how I feel, as though I'm looking at a stranger—someone with features just like mine, only relaxed, softened: someone in love, someone loved back, someone happy.

IN THE MUDROOM after the morning's landing at Cuverville Island, I hang up the extra life preservers and get ready to signal the crew to bring up the remaining Zodiac. Then I notice there's still one tag in the OFF SHIP position. I don't recognize the name, but who it is doesn't matter as much as the fact that we've left someone on shore.

"Shit," I mutter and radio Glenn to tell him to wait up.

I turn the Zodiac back toward the landing, my shoulders tensing. It's extremely rare for tourists to get left behind, and my mind flashes to Dennis. When I round the coast to the landing spot, the sight of a lone passenger standing there nearly stops me short.

"Hello?" I call out, but he doesn't seem to hear me.

I bring the Zodiac closer and call out again. "Sir, I'm here to take you back to—"

Then the red-jacketed figure turns around, taking off his hat. It's Keller.

Often during the last week of this voyage, I've felt my chest constrict at odd times—when I see Keller across the dining room during meals, when we pass each other en route to some task, when I watch him take off across the water in a Zodiac full of passengers—tense with the knowledge that, while he's here now, he'll be gone soon enough. And now, as he heads toward me, I take a long, full breath.

He wades into the water. "Permission to come aboard?" he asks.

"What exactly are you doing?" I ask, glancing backward. We're just out of sight of the ship.

"I knew you were on mudroom duty," he says, "so I made up a fake tag to lure you out here."

I shake my head, trying to look disapproving, yet I have to laugh at the sight of him bundled up in a red tourist's jacket.

"Are you *trying* to get fired during your first season? Stealing passenger clothing and going AWOL? Glenn's going to have a fit."

Keller steps into the boat. "Borrowed, not stolen. And as far as Glenn knows, you're just picking up a wayward tourist."

He puts an arm around my waist and holds me to him as he takes the helm and steers the boat out of the bay—heading not toward the ship but in the opposite direction, toward a maze of icebergs. Moments later, we're surrounded by towers and turrets of ice.

Keller loosens his hold but keeps his arm around me. "I just wanted a few minutes," he says.

He cuts the engine, and we drift.

After days of tourist chatter, of Glenn's voice on the PA, of the steady rumbling of the ship, the silence fills my mind like water in a jar—the world goes smooth and clear, with nothing but the whisk of wind around the ice, the splash of a penguin entering the water, the gurgle of waves against the ice.

We float along the edge of an iced city, the bergs rising out of the water like skyscrapers. The sea has arched doorways into the sides; the wind has chipped out windows. In the distance, several conical formations tower over the bay, with deep crevasses in their sides, as if enormous claws have slashed through them, drawing blue light instead of blood.

Keller turns his body in to mine, looking over my head at the drifting icelands beyond. Within days, even hours, these icebergs will be unrecognizable—the water will turn them around, flip them over, wash away a little more from below. The icescape we're viewing now no one's ever seen before, and no one will ever see again.

"What do you love most?" he asks.

"About you?"

He grins. "About the icebergs."

I rest my head against his shoulder for a moment before answering. "I love the way some of them look like houses. How they seem to have doors and windows and awnings and porches. It makes me want to climb inside and live in them."

"I wish we could."

He runs his hands up my arms, over my elbows to my shoulders. I want to shed my naturalist's jacket, and strip him of his tourist's coat, as he pulls me forward and kisses me, finding a slip of bare skin at the back of my neck. In the near silence, the lick of the water against the Zodiac fills my ears, and I feel as though I, too, am floating, buoyed by his hands.

Moments later, the boat lurches us back to where we are—we've drifted into view of the *Cormorant*, a dark shadow behind a thickening layer of mist, and the wind is increasing, blowing snow off the tops of the bergs.

I murmur into his neck, "We should get back."

"Not yet," he murmurs back, and as we stand in the gliding boat I sense what he's thinking: We are like the ever-shifting, ever-changing ice—and whatever happens next, wherever we end up, we'll never be quite the same again.

FIVE DAYS LATER, after disembarkation, Keller and I spend the night in an Ushuaia guesthouse, not knowing when we'll see each other next. We speak very little, even during our last moments together, when, in the sharp, bittersweet morning air, I stand with him on Calle Hernando de Magallanes as he puts his bag into the cab that will take him to the airport. He turns to me, and I press into the heat of his body, his arms around me, his fingers on my back. I want to feel the roughness of his hands one more time, his tall lean body against mine, skin to skin. I slide my hands under his pullover, landing somewhere between cotton and fleece, knowing as I do that I won't be able to reach any further, that this is as far as I can go.

FOUR DAYS BEFORE SHIPWRECK

Bransfield Strait
(62°57'S, 59°38'W)

There are no portholes in the exam room of the medical suite, and though I can feel that the sea is calm, my nausea is getting worse. I've managed to put off Glenn's insistence on a doctor's visit until today, and now I'm hoping my queasiness is only because I can't see the horizon. I know Susan has something stronger than meclizine for seasickness—she doesn't prescribe it except in extreme cases, but I'm getting to the point where I think I qualify.

I always feel a little out of sorts when I can't see the ocean—which is strange for someone who grew up in the Midwest and spends most of the year landlocked in Oregon. Growing up, I loved the water and would often swim in Shaw Park's public pool in Clayton, Missouri. I'd dive off the ten-meter platform, pretending it was a seaside cliff. I'd put on my mask and snorkel and imagine that people's limbs, in their myriad shapes and sizes, were sea creatures. I'd see their colorful swimsuits as brightly hued fish.

My other favorite place had been the geodesic dome at the botanical garden. My father used to take me there when he was in town, which wasn't often, and the rainforest inside, with its tropical humidity and mist, with waterfalls and wildly exotic plants, made me want to explore the world. By the time I was in junior high, my neighborhood had gotten one of the first outdoor-gear stores in greater St. Louis—it was a small store, but just walking through its narrow aisles felt like adventure. I'd try on the extreme-weather clothing and imagine myself at one of the poles.

I didn't know back then that I would, in fact, end up spending much of my life in one of the polar regions, and, over the years, I've come to think of the continent not only as a place but as a living, breathing thing—to me, Antarctica has always been as alive as the creatures it houses: Every winter, the entire continent fattens up with ice, then shrinks again in the summer. When I'm here on the peninsula, looking out at the green and white of young ice and the deep, ancient blue of multiyear ice, I feel as though the bergs, too, are alive, sent forth by thousands of miles of glaciers to protect the continent from such predators as the *Endurance* and the *Erebus*, the *Cormorant* and the *Australis*.

And this is what worries me.

Keller knows as well as anyone that the *Australis* isn't equipped to take on these icy sentinels. He knows what an iceberg looks like underwater, that beneath the exquisite beauty above the surface is a sharp, jagged, nasty thing that will destroy ships if they attempt to pass too close. Even for an experienced captain, miscalculating the distance is not difficult to do, with the constantly shifting winds and waters, the continual calving of new icebergs. Charts of this heavily traveled area have regions not properly surveyed, and every captain knows there is nothing more dangerous than unseen ice.

Sometimes I wonder how long this alien invasion — the ships, the humans — can continue before the continent strikes back.

Susan opens the door, returning to the closet-size examining room where I've been waiting. Earlier, she'd had me pee in a cup, had taken my vital signs and done a quick exam, asked me a dozen questions. I'm starting to feel a bit better, and I stand up as she enters the room, ready to forgo medication and be on my way.

"Have a seat," she says.

"I'm good to go, actually. Shouldn't have wasted your time."

"Please," she says, motioning me back down. Her face is serious, too serious for something like the flu.

I sit.

"Deb," she says, "I don't know if this will be good news or bad news, but" — she pauses — "you're pregnant."

"What?" I can barely choke out the word. Feebly, I lean back in the chair.

"You're pregnant."

"That's not possible."

"You mentioned that you had sex —"

"I know what I said." I can hardly think straight. "What I mean is, I was careful. Very careful. Can you run the test again?"

"Already have." Susan looks at me. I've known her for years; like so many, we see each other down here and nowhere else.

"You're going to have to take extra care on the landings. You're about eight weeks along."

She doesn't bring up options, as most doctors would, because down here there are no options for something like this.

"This can't be right," I say.

"I'm sorry," she says. She begins talking about what foods I should avoid, what activities I should let other crew members handle, but I'm barely listening. When I leave her office a few minutes later, promising I'll return, I can't remember anything she'd said.

"There you are." It's Glenn, jogging behind me in the passageway to catch up. "You all right?" he asks. "What did Susan say?"

"Don't worry," I say. "It's not food poisoning. The ship's not contaminated with norovirus. I'm fine."

"You sure about that?" He studies my face. "You don't seem yourself."

"Residual jet lag, probably. I just need a bit of rest, that's all."

He nods. "Take the rest of the day off. We don't have another landing until tomorrow. You'll probably feel better then."

I nod back, then make my way to the sanctuary of my bunk. I lie down and lay my hands across my belly, which feels the same as always. I think again of icebergs, of how much is hidden away under the surface of the water. How appearances can be so deceiving. I can conceal this pregnancy for the duration of the voyage, but then what? My mind can't move beyond this concept of ice, how everything you have to fear is what lies beneath, what's unseen and unknown.

THREE MONTHS BEFORE SHIPWRECK

Eugene, Oregon

I cross the garden from my cottage to the main house, a light rain dampening my hair. As the austral summer begins in the Southern Hemisphere, October in Oregon is much the same: gray, rainy, a chill that sinks into your bones. A few strands of hair stick to my forehead, and I pause on the back porch, securing the bottle of wine I've brought between my knees as I release my ponytail and shake out my hair, slipping the band around my wrist.

I hear the sounds of raised voices and laughter, and before I reach the door, it bursts open. "Sorry!" a woman says. The guy beside her is laughing, his arm around her waist, and they stumble out into the garden.

As usual, I'm late to the party and a bit too sober.

For the last five years, I've rented the little cottage behind this restored Craftsman where my landlord-now-friend Nick Atwood lives with a fluffy white cat named Gatsby. Nick and I basically share custody of Gatsby—Nick's an entomologist at the university, and his house is so often filled with colleagues and friends that Gatsby frequently comes to my place for some peace and quiet.

Nick's kitchen is warm and smells of his famous Brazilian risotto cakes. I put the wine on the counter. Gatsby comes over, tail in the air, and lets me scratch him behind the ears. "What're you still doing here?" I ask him. "I expected you at my place hours ago." He flicks his tail and stalks into the laundry room.

I head toward the living room and immediately bump into Nick, who's on his way to the kitchen. He gives me a big hug, and a kiss somewhere around my ear. "I was about to give up on you."

"Sorry. Traffic was brutal."

"Right."

Nick draws me into a circle of colleagues and their plus-ones; he slips a brimming wineglass into my hand, makes introductions, and leaves me with the group. I wish for a few familiar faces, like my friend Jill, a fellow bio lecturer who's away visiting her boyfriend in San Francisco. It's much more fun when she and I can be each other's date for the evening amid all the couples.

"So *you're* Deb," says a professor from Nick's department.

I turn to look at her—a dark-haired woman named Sydney, sharp-featured but soft-eyed, her slender body standing very straight. "Have we met before?" I ask.

"No," Sydney says. "But I've heard a lot about you."

Before I can ask what she's talking about, she introduces me to her boyfriend, a construction manager who draws us into a discussion about LEED-certified building and local politics. I listen, trying not to think about how I'm neglecting the lesson plans for my biology course. Eventually I ease my way out of the conversation and wander across the room.

The house is neat and clean, with Nick's love of invertebrates on full display; the walls in the living room are covered with photographs and illustrations of bees and butterflies. As much as I dislike parties, I do like the white noise of them, and I always enjoy being in Nick's house. I love seeing the way he's merged science with art, and I like the semisocial aspect of being around people, even if not fully engaged with them.

Soon I feel the draft of Nick's front door opening and closing, the noise level in the room fading slowly as the party winds down. As I turn the corner into the empty hallway, the ambient sounds of people talking and laughing and saying good night are almost like a lullaby.

The first time Nick invited me over, soon after I'd moved into the cottage, I demurred—as I did the second and third times. Finally, to be polite, I went, feeling the whole time as though I were in a dollhouse, as if I were back home, where my mother's eagle eye would catch every fingerprint I left, every speck of dirt my shoes deposited on the floor. Then one of his friends toppled a glass of wine onto the couch, staining its beige cushion with a large, deep-crimson moon—and Nick simply poured her a fresh glass and tossed a pillow over the stain. *Trust me, Gatsby's done a lot worse to that couch*, he said.

That's when I began to relax—once I noticed the claw marks on the coffee table, the shredded arm of the sofa, the tiny nose prints on the inside of the kitchen window. And over the years, as we've grown closer, Nick has become one of the few constants in my life, someone who's always here when I come home after months away.

Now I wander back into the kitchen, where Nick's talking to Sydney. Her boyfriend isn't around, and they don't see me, and I feel, as I often do in these situations, that I'm not really a part of what's happening but observing it from a distant place; I'm on the periphery, like something in the background of a photograph that never catches the untrained eye.

When the boyfriend returns, we say our good nights. Nick walks them both to the front door, his hand brushing against my back as he passes by.

I open the dishwasher and begin to run water over the glasses in the sink. A few minutes later, Nick is back, depositing empty beer bottles into the recycle bin in the corner.

"Leave it for the maid!" he says, pouring himself another glass of wine.

"I would, if you actually had a maid."

He leans over to shut off the water, gently hip-butting me out of the way. I see that he's used a rubber band to tie his hair—a thick, light-brown mop he never seems to know what to do with—into a little bob at the nape of his neck.

"Come here a second," I say.

I stand behind him and begin to untangle the dirty rubber band from his hair, as gently as I can. He tilts his head back to help, and I feel the waver of his inebriated body trying hard to stand still. I pull my ponytail holder from my wrist and put it between my teeth, running my hands through his hair, smoothing it out. It's a little damp from the rain outside, and it smells green, like a forest. I pull the hair back and tie it behind his head again. Then I turn him around to face me. "No more rubber bands," I tell him. "They tear the shit out of your hair."

"I'm thinking of cutting it, actually," Nick says, running his hand along the back of his head.

"Don't," I say. "It looks good long."

"Really?"

"Sure." His hair, especially when it's tousled, reminds me of Keller's.

He looks as if he's about to ask me something, but he doesn't. Nick has a sweet face, like a Saint Bernard's: calm, competent, a little somber. He's tall and solidly built, and with his year-round suntan, from studying insects up and down the West Coast, he looks more like a rugby player than an entomologist.

As I sneak a couple of glasses into the dishwasher, I say, "That professor friend of yours, Sydney—what have you told her about me?"

"Nothing."

"She said she's heard a lot about me."

"That's what friends do," he says. "We talk from time to time."

"About what?"

"Why you never come to my parties. Despite the fact that I'm an excellent cook and you have nothing but dehydrated camping food in your house."

"I'm here. Fashionably late, but here."

"You know what I mean," he says. "When would I ever see you, if I didn't drag you over here for food and booze?"

"I'd bring the rent check by eventually."

"Funny," he says.

"Oh, you know I'm kidding."

"Right. Because you pay by direct deposit."

"It's not that."

"It is, though, isn't it?" He props himself against the counter. "Don't you ever go out?"

"Sure I do," I say. "Just the other night, Jill and I went out to Sam Bond's to grade quizzes."

"Doing work at the local pub is still working," he says.

"We had beer."

"Unless you woke up in someone else's bed with a raging hangover, it doesn't count."

"For the record," I say, "I *do* have a social life. He just doesn't live here. In Oregon, I mean."

Nick raises his eyebrows. "I'm familiar with the concept of long-distance relationships," he says, "but don't you think that's a little extreme?"

"You're one to talk, Professor Kettle. I don't recall seeing any single women at this party."

"I thought you counted penguins for a living."

"Your point?"

"You counted wrong." He steps closer. "But then, she was the last one to arrive."

I reach for a nearby wine bottle and refill my glass because I don't know what to say.

"Remember what Freud said?" he asks. "You need two things in life—love and work. You know, as in a balance of the two?"

"Maybe I like being off-balance."

He takes a step backward, still slouched against the counter, as if holding himself up. "I'm serious. When are you going to settle down? Join the real world?"

"Come on, Nick—you're a scientist. Reality's depressing."